STRANGERS IN SAVANNAH

THE SOUTHERN SLEUTH BOOK 5

HARPER LIN

CHAPTER 1

*I*t was one of those heavy afternoons when the temperature hadn't quite hit one hundred, but it felt like it. There wasn't the slightest breeze. Not a single leaf on any of the tobacco plants on the MacKenzie tobacco plantation stirred. The sky was a sharp, crisp blue devoid of even a small puffy white cloud that could provide a temporary relief from the scorching sun.

"My goodness, this heat is enough to make me want to strip off my clothes and go for a dip in Klein's pond," Becky MacKenzie said as she took a seat on the porch swing. The finger curls of her red hair were loose; no amount of pomade was going to hold them in place.

Kitty MacKenzie gasped. "Rebecca Madeline. I'll not have my daughter saying such scandalous things. Why, if the wrong fellow heard you saying that, he might just take you up on the offer. Then where would you be?"

"Oh, Mama. For heaven's sake. I'd be down at Klein's pond feeling cool and content," Becky replied with a sly smirk. Of course, she'd never do anything of the sort. At least not with a stranger. But she did love to antagonize her mother. Kitty was always trying to find a husband for Becky, and even the oppressive heatwave that had swept over Savannah for the past few days hadn't slowed her efforts.

"I do hope you aren't going to talk like that when Herbert Coleman arrives. His mother has told me that he's been very much looking forward to meeting you," Kitty replied with her own sly grin as she peeked over the top of the newspaper she'd been reading.

That was enough to change Becky's expression from snarky to serious. She looked out at the long rows of tobacco. If it wasn't so hot, she would have liked to go and lose herself in the rows for a day or two. Certainly, long enough to miss her engagement with Herbert Coleman.

She'd been hearing about the man for the past week and his long, impressive list of attributes. Herbert was from a prominent family from Raleigh. He branched out on his own and landed a job with a metal factory, where he'd quickly climbed the ropes. He might not have been the handsomest man in Raleigh, but there were a number of young ladies from the upper echelon that were hot on his heels. Becky should be thrilled he was coming to meet her specifically. The thought made her stomach fold over on itself.

"I doubt I'll have much to say at all," Becky replied, her voice hushed. The last thing she wanted was to be short with her mother. She knew her intentions were good, but this was too soon for Becky. Going out with her friends was one thing. A date? A date she knew was going to fall flat? It was exhausting just to think about it.

"Becky, dear, I know you are still thinking of that other young man." Kitty lowered the paper and looked at her daughter, tilting her head slightly to the left.

"His name was Adam White, Mama. You know that," Becky replied softly.

"Yes. Adam White. Truth be told, I did like him.

3

He wasn't exactly what I'd hoped for for my daughter, but he made you happy. However…" Kitty took a deep breath. "He isn't making you happy now. He's left after making a fool of himself with another girl."

"I know what he did, Mama. I don't need to be reminded." Becky rolled her eyes.

"I'm sorry, honey. I just hate to see you sulking. Herbert has promised to take you out for a wonderful time. He's got a good job with a company that makes beds for prisons. Isn't that fascinating?"

It had been several weeks since Adam left town. It was as Kitty had said. He'd stepped out on Becky with an unknown woman, and now that Becky knew about it, she didn't want to see him anymore. It wasn't that she wasn't heartbroken. She was. Devastated, in fact. But there was that part of her, the part that ached and pushed tears into her eyes and made her tired five minutes after she got up in the morning, that still wanted to see him. That part wanted to hold on and pretend nothing had changed. But even if there was a way she could forgive Adam's indiscretion, even if they could make a go of things again, he was gone.

"Yes, Mama. Fascinating."

"And I've heard he's the youngest man in the company to already become a foreman. That means he's got several men working beneath him. He knows how to take charge. That's a good quality for a man to have," Kitty continued.

"I'm all right, Mama," Becky insisted.

"You might be all right, but you're not yourself. I think a good time with a new fella will do you a world of wonders. A change is as good as a rest," Kitty insisted before going back to her paper. After a few minutes of quiet between her and her daughter, Kitty said, "Oh dear."

Just then, Cousin Fanny walked out of the house and took a seat next to Becky, stirring the air with a white, lacy fan.

"Mama, it's impolite to gasp when a person enters the room. Even if it is Fanny," Becky teased. Her cousin Fanny annoyed her. Throughout their whole lives, she found Cousin Fanny to be a *pain* in the fanny.

"Rebecca, you know darn well I wasn't gasping at Fanny," Kitty replied with a sigh.

"Don't worry about me, Aunt Kitty. Children often lash out when they feel jealous or insecure," Fanny replied before clearing her throat and smoothing out her skirt.

"I am not jealous." Becky rolled her eyes again. If she had to be honest, she might then admit she was slightly envious of her cousin, who had more than enough cleavage for the entire city of Savannah to enjoy.

"Hush, you two. I was gasping because there was another dead person found," Kitty said, shaking her head. "This time, it was on North Bryn Mawr Street. My goodness."

"Another beheading?" Becky leaned forward. "That would make the third one this month. Do they know the name of the victim?"

Kitty shook her head. "No. Another transient. As if those people don't have enough to worry about. It's a dangerous life. But this one was found near the railroad tracks. Seems the police believe he might have fallen asleep and didn't hear the train come by. Oh, how awful."

"I know when I was in Paris, you saw nary a bum. It's just a much cleaner city. Why, if I had to guess, I'd say some of the knockabouts on Avenue Montaigne were more certified than your brightest professor from Savannah," Fanny replied while still fanning her face.

"I can't read anymore," Kitty said as she stood, the wicker seat making a crinkling sound. "I have letters to write. You girls behave out here. It's too hot for any shenanigans."

Becky snatched up the paper, unfolded it to maximum capacity, and held it in front of her face to block out her cousin. It worked. For a moment. Just as she started to read the article about the death of the latest member of Savannah's homeless population, she heard Fanny's voice cut through her peace like the drip-drip-drip of a faucet at midnight.

"I'm trying to read," Becky replied.

"I do hope you aren't going to bring up this gruesome development with your date tomorrow. Aunt Kitty is desperate to have you snap out of this depression. Do you have any idea what you are doing to her? Why, she barely wants to go into town and leave you alone. It's quite selfish, Becky," Fanny said, her fan never ceasing.

"You only want her to go downtown because you know she'll buy you something. Do you really think she's not on to your flim-flam?" Becky kept her voice low but her words sharp.

"That isn't true. But even if it were, I'm not going to insult my aunt's kind gestures and refuse her generosity."

"Of course, Fanny. You've never refused anyone's gestures, kind or otherwise, from what I've heard." Becky clammed up as Moxley stepped out on the porch. The sight of him brought an instant smile to her face. He'd been the MacKenzies' butler for as long as Becky could remember. There was a stability when Moxley was around. He brought as much of a sense of comfort as her father did.

"Good morning, ladies," he said as he crossed the porch.

"Good morning, Moxley. Did you get a chance to read the paper?" Becky asked.

"Yes, ma'am," he replied as he adjusted the seats to take advantage of the shade as the sun crept across the front of the house.

"Did you see there was another dead body found? I think it's murder," Becky continued as her cousin rolled her eyes.

"They ain't calling it murder. They say another accident. T'ain't a safe place to be for those poor souls," Moxley said.

"A string of unhappy coincidences." Becky looked at Moxley then down at the paper. "What do you think?"

"I think I'm glad for a roof over my head, Miss Becky. Would you ladies like some sweet tea while you're chatting?" he asked innocently, but Becky knew better and squinted at the glint of mischief in her butler's eye. He knew how she felt about Fanny, but like a good house servant, Moxley never said it out loud.

"No thank you, Moxley. I do believe I need to soak in the tub for a while," Fanny replied. "Would you tell Lucretia to draw a bath for me?"

"Yes, ma'am," Moxley replied with a nod. "You sure about that sweet tea, Miss Becky? It just got a little sweeter."

"Fine, Moxley. If you insist." Becky grinned before going back to her paper as Fanny got up from the swing. "Don't forget to soak your head."

"Very funny," Fanny snapped before stepping inside.

Once the porch was empty and the icy glass of sweet tea was at her side, Becky tried to focus on the article in the paper. The latest transient death was on Bryn Mawr Street. She knew that street well and hadn't been there in a while. Once the sun started to set, she decided she'd go downtown to see what was happening. When Herbert Coleman arrived tomorrow, she was going to have no time to herself.

As much as she hated to admit it, Becky was looking forward to a distraction from her breakup with Adam. She was tired of being sad, yet she felt there was no way to stop it except to go through it. She and Adam had been seeing each other on the sly for quite some time. He wasn't wealthy or prominent. But when he finally met Judge and Kitty MacKenzie, he held his head high and made Becky proud. To her, the ink beneath his nails from the printing presses where he worked was no different from the medals a four-star general would have on his uniform. Was she blinded by his good looks? Did she lose her head over him to such an extent that she didn't see the warning signs? Had things changed once he was no longer a secret?

"Maybe that was it. Maybe once the game of keeping our relationship under wraps was over, he lost interest," she muttered. When she stood, Becky pulled at the fabric of her dress, which had been sticking to her back. After standing on the porch, thinking of nothing, Becky decided she didn't want to be alone. Looking over her shoulder to the front door, she saw her mother busy at her writing table. There were letters to relatives and friends that needed to be sent. It was important to keep in touch, Kitty would always say. Quietly, Becky tiptoed into the house and upstairs to her room. Fanny could be heard in the bathroom singing "Ain't Misbehavin'" off-key while soaking in the tub. Once in her room, Becky shut the door, grabbed her sketchbook and pencils, and shimmied down the trellis. She hadn't left the house like this in weeks. It didn't feel the same. Becky feared her breakup with Adam was forcing maturity on her. As much as her heart was aching, this fact made her angry. She wasn't ready for full-blown adulthood yet. Without her realizing it, her pace had quickened as she made her way to Old Brick Cemetery, which was at the edge of her family's property.

Taking up her favorite spot beneath the canopy of mossy drapes surrounded by the crumbling and neglected tombstones of those who came before her, Becky began to sketch random doodles.

"Well, look who it is," she heard a familiar voice say. When she looked up, she saw Mr. Wilcox. Just the person she was hoping to see.

"Hello, Mr. Wilcox. Care to sit a spell with me?" she asked and scooted over to make room at the base of the huge shade tree.

"Don't mind if I do. I haven't seen you around these parts for a while. Those Yankees keeping you from paying me a visit?" he asked, his face suddenly grim and serious. He hadn't forgiven the Yankees for the War of Northern Aggression.

"No, sir. I do believe the Yankees have all but abandoned Savannah. They didn't expect our fine Southern gentlemen to put up such a fight," Becky said with a smile to her ghostly friend. Mr. Wilcox had died shortly after the Civil War. But he'd decided he wasn't ready to see Jesus and instead roamed the property butted against the MacKenzie plantation, chatting with the other permanent residents of Old Brick Cemetery and Becky.

It was a gift Becky'd had her whole life. She often saw things, people that no one else could. At first it was scary. However, in time she learned that people, alive or dead, just wanted to be listened to.

"So, if it wasn't those Northerners keeping you, what was it?" Mr. Wilcox asked as he took a seat in the shade next to Becky. Before Becky could form the words, her eyes filled with tears. The story about Adam just spilled out.

"I guess it really was a Northerner keeping me from here." She chuckled bitterly once she'd finished her tale of woe.

Mr. Wilson stroked his gray beard, flicked the tips of his mustache, then cleared his throat. "I'm sorry you've suffered such scandal, my dear. You can cry if you need to."

Although she couldn't hug Mr. Wilcox or hold his hand, Becky was more grateful to him for giving her permission to weep than for all the advice in the world. Her heart needed it. So she accepted his invitation and cried. Despite all the advice and suggestions she'd gotten from the living, it was a dead man who understood her pain. Once she'd shed all her tears, she wiped her eyes and let out a deep sigh.

CHAPTER 2

By the time the sun had disappeared behind the horizon and the moon began a game of peek-a-boo from behind a few scattered clouds, Becky was feeling a little more like herself. But that also might have had to do with the company she was keeping. Or the music that was playing. Or maybe the hooch they were drinking

"Becky, you are my very best friend. I would never lie to you," Martha Bourdeaux shouted with a slight slur over the band playing.

"I know that, Martha," Becky called back as she watched all the couples dancing, her foot tapping to the beat. She'd been on the dance floor with a couple of palookas, but tonight was a night to watch the scenery.

"I'm just going to come right out and sing. Adam White was no good for you." Martha put her right hand on her hip and looked straight at Becky with heavy-lidded eyes.

"What? You're smoked. You liked Adam, and you know it. That's just the sauce talking. I might have to tell Teddy to ease up on the bathtub gin," Becky replied as she patted Martha's hand. They two young ladies had grown up together, since their mothers were the best of friends.

There wasn't a secret between the two of them.

"Yes. Yes. Maybe so. But I'm going to spit it out. Adam was the cat's pajamas, but I don't know if I can forgive him for collecting some Sheba when he's practically handcuffed to you. I was supposed to be your maid of honor at your wedding, and Teddy would be... the best man or... maybe the flower girl," Martha slurred before both girls erupted in a fit of laughter.

"I'm sure the love of your life would be tickled to hear you talking about him like this." Becky shook her head. She hadn't drunk as much as Martha had. There wouldn't be a whole lot of hammering going on in her head the following morning. Instead, Becky was having a pleasant time watching everyone else. It seemed the whole room was alive with excitement, and everyone had a date or two, a drink in their hand, and a bounce in their step. Even if she hadn't felt like it, Becky was glad she was out.

"It's just that you're my best friend." Martha started to get teary-eyed. "I hate to see you like this."

"You're daft! I'm having a swell time. I always do with you," Becky soothed. "Heck, I'm not even all that annoyed with Fanny being here."

"She's got a couple of weak sisters at the bar. You'd think some of the Brunos would catch on to her schtick by now, but…" Martha tossed back the last of her champagne cocktail.

"They never do." Becky felt that twinge of jealousy in the middle of her chest and tossed back a swig of her own champagne cocktail to drown it out.

The music shifted from bouncy to smooth when the band began "Moonlight Serenade," and out of nowhere Teddy appeared, offering his elbow to his favorite gal.

"Can I have this dance?" Teddy asked Martha. Although he'd grown up in the house next door to Becky, Theodore Penbroke's heart always had and always would belong to Martha Bourdeaux.

"You're just the bee's knees, Teddy," Martha replied, took hold of his arm, and stood from the table. It was amazing to Becky how quickly Martha could regain her composure when Teddy was around. As she watched them sashay to the dance floor and slip in between with all the other lovers holding one another tight, she couldn't help but feel the melancholy that had settled in.

"This is getting ridiculous," she muttered before tossing back the last of her drink.

After her cry with Mr. Wilcox, she was happy to be at Willie's club. It was her home away from home. She'd be hard-pressed to find anyone who didn't know her, if not by name, at least by sight. The loud music and dim lights gave her just enough cover to hide the puffiness that remained around her eyes and drown out the news that broke her heart, which kept playing on loop in her head.

"Excuse me." A male voice caused Becky to turn around.

"Yes?" she said before finding herself face-to-face with a portly gent with twinkling blue eyes and a head full of thick, wavy blond hair.

"I saw you come in," he said.

Becky smiled. Although she wasn't interested in striking up a new romance immediately, her confidence was grateful for the bump. She extended her hand but prepared to let him down gently.

"Becky MacKenzie," she said over the music.

"Uh, er, hi, Becky. You came in with that blonde at the bar. What can you tell me about her?" the man asked as his gaze zeroed in on Fanny, who was doing what she always did—flapping her gums and flipping her hair while pretending she didn't know what she looked like. Without her realizing it, Becky's shoulders drooped.

"What can I tell you about *her*? Well—" Becky cleared her throat and for a split second considered telling this gent her cousin was fascinated with butchers and the habits of monkeys. "She loves Paris."

The man snapped his fingers, winked at Becky, and gave her a nudge on the chin. "Thanks, doll." He straightened his tie, smoothed his hair, and strolled confidently to the bar to slip between Fanny and the big gorilla who had been buying her drinks most of the night.

"Well, that's just applesauce," Becky huffed. So much for her ego getting a much-needed boost. Feeling awkward and annoyed, she got up from the table and marched herself to the opposite end of the bar from Fanny and waved down the bartender.

"Champagne cocktail," she shouted. Within seconds, she had a fresh sparkling glass of bubbly in her hand. She took a quick sip before glancing in

Fanny's direction. Sure enough, there was a tussle starting where Fanny was sitting.

But as Becky made her way back to the table, she realized another man had joined the circus. Just as things started to get louder and some shoving started, Teddy and Martha left the dance floor and stood with Becky.

"What's that all about?" Martha asked.

"Some buster put himself behind the eight ball trying to get in Fanny's good graces. That alderman decided that palooka was no match for him and squeezed him out. Poor sap is gonna find himself staring down the business end of a peashooter if he isn't careful," Becky said as she took her seat and smoothed out the frill of her skirt.

"No," Teddy replied. "It looks more serious than that."

When Becky looked up, she saw a whole lot of commotion. It looked like something was rippling its way through the crowd. People were stepping back, making room as the doormen pushed and shoved in pursuit of a rummy from the neighborhood.

"Looks like he's on a bender," Martha said as she cozied closer to Teddy more out of fear than affection. Becky stared. The man didn't belong in Willie's looking the way he did.

"Maybe someone slipped him a Mickey Finn," Teddy offered. But as Becky watched, he maneuvered through the crowd, slipping away from the entrance goons at every turn, ducking in one spot only to pop up in another.

"If someone did, he's the most coordinated drunk I've ever seen," Becky replied as she watched the scene unfold. At first, she was sure that there was nothing more going on than a jingle-brained jobbie who was causing a scene. But it only took a matter of seconds before she realized there was more to this performance than met the eye. In fact, it was the dead-on look from this vagabond that made Becky feel as though someone had just walked over her grave. He spotted her, and like a crab scurrying across the sand to get away from a diving gull, made a beeline to their table.

Teddy pushed Martha behind him and was about to step in front of the table when the man reached it.

"You can't hide! They've already found you!" He shook as he spoke.

Up close, Becky could smell the whiskey on his breath mixed with the smell of stale clothes that had been worn for several days in a row. His eyes were bloodshot, and the skin beneath them looked thin, like draped lace curtains. His hair was short. Judging by its asymmetrical appearance, there was a high probability that the man had cut it himself. His hands were rough from grabbing onto the hot, hard metal sides of train cars as he rode the rails from place to place. The man didn't look like anything more than a wire hanger with oversized clothes hanging from it, but before she could make a move, he snatched up her hand in his, squeezed it tight, and would not let go.

In a flash, Becky was frozen. She didn't know if it was shock or if she was under a spell. It didn't really matter, since the transient had her by the hand. She could feel hard calluses, and they were hot, like he might have had a fever.

"They've already found you, and you'll lose your head next! You'll lose your head next! Do you hear me? They can see you!" the man was shouting at Becky, but there was a glaze over his eyeballs. No one could be sure he was seeing anything but the pink elephants prancing in front of him—a result of the delirium from not having enough to drink.

That was what the gawkers and onlookers thought. Just a rummy on the bends. But Becky was seeing something different altogether.

In a flash of bright light as quick as lightning, the dance hall transformed into a dark cave with more shadows than light, and all the revelers gathered around her. Some were laughing. Others were talking but making no sense with words she couldn't make out. But then there were some who were not just mad but enraged, glaring down at her like hungry animals.

Over the past several months, Becky had been experiencing this kind of altered state in small episodes. Her mother would hiss horribly cruel things to her only to snap back to the loving, dedicated woman Becky had grown up with. Her father had done the same. Martha and Teddy had slipped into a strange episode of criticizing her, as well as Fanny. Although Becky had to admit Fanny might have actually been criticizing her, Martha and Teddy, never. It was all baloney. Hallucinations. Daydreams that were more vivid than Becky had expected. But this was something altogether different. She didn't have a clue who half the people who were scowling at her were. The others who were laughing and chatting acted like Becky wasn't even there, like she was invisible.

"They know where you are and what you can do, and you'll be next! You're going to lose your head!

Lose your head!" the bum screamed so loud his body shook, and the veins popped on his head and neck. Becky looked away for fear his eyeballs were going to pop right out of their sockets. Finally, she felt the warm touch of something on her hand. Like she was being yanked back from falling off a cliff, everything snapped back into place. Becky gasped, taking a gulp of air as if she'd been underwater the whole time.

"You better turn tail, pal!" Teddy shouted at the hobo, who shrank into himself, no longer the crazed wild man he'd been but rather a confused older man who seemed to not quite have his wits about him. Two sets of mitts clamped down on the man's shoulders as the doormen finally caught up to him.

"You're out of here!" they shouted as they pulled the man roughly through the crowd. Everyone stood back, giving the trio safe passage from the dance floor to the entrance. The bum was probably going to get a working over before everything was said and done. But as far as Becky could see, they were tossing the man out like they were throwing out the trash. For some reason, she felt bad.

"Becky, are you all right?" Martha squeezed her hand and looked up at Teddy.

"Come on, Rebecca. Snap out of it," Teddy encouraged. "Here. A little hair of the dog." A champagne cocktail appeared in front of her nose. Becky grasped the glass in both hands and swallowed the whole drink. The bubbles raced up her nose, making her eyes water, and within seconds, she burped.

"Excuse me," she replied. "What in the world just happened?"

"Oh, thank goodness! I was afraid that hobo had put the whammy on you. He was out on the roof!" Martha said, looking back and forth between Becky and Teddy.

"He was off the track. A real head case. Well, it's rough out there for some people. They think the whole world is out to get them," Teddy replied before lifting Becky's face with his finger under her chin. "Let's get one more round and call it a night."

"That sounds ducky. One more round will do us both some good," Martha replied, still holding on to Becky's hand. "You gave me a real fright. I was sure you were going to pull back and deck that number. He'd have had it coming for sure."

"You thought I was going to hit him?"

"The look on your face wasn't one of a shrinking violet, I'll say that much. What did he say to you? It was impossible to hear over this crowd." Martha looked worried. Before Becky could censor herself, the words just tumbled out.

"He said they found me, and I was going to lose my head," Becky replied as she looked around the joint.

"What?" Martha gasped. "That's a load of horse-feathers. Obviously, he's pickled and doesn't know what he's saying. Speaking of which, here comes Teddy. Get a load of the waiter we've got."

Becky looked up and saw Teddy with a drink in each hand and one balancing on his head. She couldn't help but smile. Still, as she took her glass and Martha told Teddy what the bum had said, Becky was feeling different. It was a weird jumble of feelings that were all fighting to bubble to the surface. She took her glass, toasted her friends absently, then gulped the drink down. Her hands trembled slightly, but she kept them under the table as she forced herself into the conversation with Teddy and Martha.

"What's going on over here?" Fanny asked as she wiggled herself snugly into the seat next to Teddy. Martha looked at Becky and rolled her eyes. For the first time in a long time, Becky couldn't find a clever retort resting at the tip of her tongue.

"You didn't see all the commotion?" Teddy asked.

"Commotion? No. In case you hadn't noticed, I was chatting with a couple of gents at the bar. One of them was about to ask me on a date when a rude fatty interrupted everything, trying to get me to dance," Fanny huffed. Becky suddenly remembered the guy who had asked about her cousin.

"He looked like a fine gent. Why didn't you dance with him? Afraid you might break one or more of his toes?" She felt a little better after that zinger, but there was still something loitering around in her head that she couldn't quite shake.

"Very funny. It isn't my fault all of you stomp around and call it dancing. I'm just more familiar with the dances in Paris. They are a little more... refined." Fanny patted her hair in place.

Becky was about to reply, opening her mouth and pointing her finger, when Teddy swooped in. "Yeah, well, we were about to call it a night. I'm spent," he said, stretching his arms out wide and yawning.

"Yeah. Mama's got plans for us to visit... s-some-one... tomorrow," Martha stuttered. She was never very good at lying. That was one of her best qualities. "I've got to hit the sack too."

"If you all want to be a bunch of party poopers. The only one with plans tomorrow is Becky when Mr. Coleman arrives. What will you two be doing? I'm sure Aunt Kitty has devised a wonderful itinerary for the two of you to get to know one another." Fanny smirked.

"We'll all be filled in on the rumble once it's all done. Let's skedaddle," Teddy interrupted.

There were very few things that would shake Becky after a confrontation like she'd just had with the hobo. Why, she'd been experiencing *the strange* since her days in her crib and had grown pretty good at keeping her emotions in check. But one word out of her cousin Fanny's mouth was enough to send her over the moon. Especially when it came to being fixed up by her mother.

"I can already predict what will happen," Martha chimed in, sounding much more sober than she had just a short while earlier. "Herbert Coleman will be smitten with Becky. She won't have the slightest interest. The end."

"I don't know what you're waiting for, Rebecca," Fanny continued. "One of these days, there won't be any more suitors to fix you up with. Your youth will disappear just like Adam did."

Becky clenched her fists. But Teddy came to the rescue. He stepped in front of her, slipped his arm around her waist, nearly picking her up completely off the floor, and to the beat of the band, titupped her to the door.

"Easy, girl," he spoke in her ear.

"One of these days. Teddy, I'm going to lay her flat. What is it with me that I attract the worst of the worst?" Becky sighed.

"I beg your pardon?"

"You know what I mean. This bum tonight. Fanny? Aside from you and Martha, I'm a charity case."

Teddy finally dropped Becky on solid ground once they were outside. "That mac didn't know what he was saying or who he was looking at. Fanny? Since when do you care what Miss Paris Puss has to say?"

"I don't care, but sometimes..."

"I have an idea. Prove Fanny wrong. Go out tomorrow with Mr. Herbert, looking to have a swell time. Hey, if nothing else, it'll be a free meal and a couple of drinks. You've already come out in the lead," Teddy said. "And who knows, Beck. You might find a guy—not to marry but someone who is just as ducky over you as I am."

Becky gave him a peck on the cheek. "You're a good egg, Teddy."

"Yes. That I am," he said as Martha emerged from the club.

"That's all I'm saying." Martha was obviously in

the middle of a conversation and had to lower her voice since they were outside.

"It isn't my fault," Fanny replied.

"Well, fine. You've said more than enough," Martha continued.

"I'm nothing if not honest," Fanny continued.

Her last comment caused a sideways glance from the entire group, but no one challenged anything. Becky was annoyed but had to admit she was worn out. The evening didn't turn out the way she'd hoped. But one thing was certain. Over the past half hour, she hadn't thought of Adam once.

CHAPTER 3

*a*s hard as it was to take Teddy's advice, Becky was determined to be as pleasant as punch to Herbert when he arrived. She had several questions she had rehearsed to keep the conversation going, and she wore one of her prettiest afternoon dresses. It gave Cousin Fanny a run for her money, since it dipped scandalously deeper than Becky's typical daytime clothes and was easily flounced by the slightest breeze, showing her figure and legs, which were perfectly toned from all her nights of dancing. When she looked in the mirror, she was thrilled.

"You clean up pretty well, Rebecca," she said to her reflection. Just then there was a knock on her bedroom door.

"Yes," she called.

The door opened carefully, and Lucretia, their maid, peeked her head in. "There is a Mr. Herbert Coleman here to see you. My, my, my... Miss Becky, you look... why, you look like you just stepped out of your mama's *McCall's* magazine."

"You think so?" Becky said, doing a quick twirl.

"I do. If Mr. Herbert takes you anywhere, he might have to swat the other fellows aside if he wants to keep you," Lucretia replied, smiling wide.

"Thanks, Lucy. I'm thinking of making the best of this one. Maybe Kitty picked a winner," Becky said in a whisper.

"Oh, Miss Becky, you are bad." Lucretia chuckled as she shut the door. Becky gave herself one more once-over, curtsied to her reflection, then grabbed her clutch purse and headed downstairs. It took her all morning to get ready and feel confident. It took a matter of seconds for it all to be crushed.

"I don't believe this," Becky said as she looked at the portly man with the thick, wavy blond hair and twinkling blue eyes who had asked about Fanny the night before.

"Well, hello," he said looking Becky up and down. "I am hoping that you are Rebecca."

"This is a fine how-do-you-do. You were asking

me about my cousin last night. Remember?" Becky
put her hand on her hip. As she watched Herbert
Coleman stand there with his mouth hanging open
like he was trying to catch flies, the desire to slap
him across the face washed over her.

"That was you?"

Becky's right eyebrow arched, and she took two
steps up to him. It was obvious what he was trying
to look at while remaining somewhat gentlemanly.
Becky wasn't one to flaunt every curve, like her
cousin did. But at this moment, she felt like a Sheba.

"Oh my, Miss Rebecca. I was rolled over is all.
Sometimes I lose myself when the band starts playing. There weren't too many dames to dance with,
and when that happens, well, Old Herbert has the
tendency to hit the sauce a little hard," he said in one
breath while sliding his right hand along the side of
his head, smoothing his hair.

Just then, like clockwork, Fanny came galloping
down the stairs in one of her most figure-enhancing
dresses, acting like she'd forgotten company was
arriving for Becky.

"I'm so sorry, cousin. I forgot you were entertaining and..." Her eyes bugged for a moment before
a sly grin slipped across her lips. "Why, I know you.
You're the buster who asked me to dance last night.

I'm so sorry I had to turn you down. You see, I'd already promised the next dance to the gent I was standing with and..."

"It's all copacetic," he said politely, but his eyes traveled back to Becky instantly.

"Herbert, this is my cousin Fanny. Fanny, I believe you already know Herbert Coleman," Becky said and walked over to the love seat, where a pitcher of sweet tea was glistening on the table. She needed a drink and would have preferred something a little stronger, but then she thought, *Any port in a storm*. She poured herself a glass and took a seat.

Fanny cleared her throat noisily and put her hand gently on Herbert's arm before he could follow Becky and take a seat.

"I don't think we were properly introduced. It is my pleasure completely." Fanny offered her hand. Herbert shook it quickly then immediately shuffled over to Becky.

"May I sit down?" he asked.

Becky hated to admit it, but she was liking the attention. Of course, she was playing another character, not quite herself. Normally, she'd painfully tolerate her dates by entertaining their random conversations, trying to act interested in what they had to say. She'd be polite. But today, with Herbert

Coleman sitting there and Fanny trying desperately to get back his attention, which she dismissed yesterday, Becky was feeling fresh. She motioned for him to take a seat.

"My mama says you're a real butter and egg man," Becky said without batting an eye. Herbert didn't seem to mind. In fact, the grin on his face as he took a seat was the most self-satisfied look she'd seen since the last time Fanny got a new dress.

"I must admit I do all right." He looked her up and down. "But I have to say, Mrs. MacKenzie did not inform me that her daughter was so breathtaking."

Becky handed him a glass of sweet tea. "Here. It'll help you cool off."

She didn't know where such a remark came from, but she liked the way it took Herbert by surprise. A little part of her was tired of being polite. What had it gotten her but a broken heart? As strange as it was, Herbert gave off a vibe that convinced Becky he really could be some fun. That might be just what she needed.

"Why, Rebecca. That's no way to talk to our guest." Fanny gasped and struck a pose against the piano that would have made Lillian Gish green with envy. "Please forgive my cousin, Mr. Coleman. She's…"

"No need for apology. I like a girl with spunk, and Rebecca, you're stove up with it." Herbert smiled before taking a sip of tea. "I've got tickets to the main event in town. What do you say we paint the town red? Have a couple of steaks for supper, go watch the fights, and then maybe a little dancing. You do dance, don't you, Rebecca?"

"I do. A little," she lied. Of course, she loved to dance.

"Well, whatever steps you don't know, you will by this time tomorrow. How about it?" Becky looked at Fanny, who was pretending not to listen even though she was leaning so far over in their direction, she looked like a pained palm tree bending against hurricane winds.

"I think it sounds swell," Becky replied.

"Hotsy-totsy. Tell your mama I do appreciate the invitation to lunch but that you and I will be off to the races this evening." Herbert winked, making Becky smile reluctantly. Even though they hadn't started off on good terms, Herbert was quickly becoming more and more fascinating.

"Rebecca, you forget that you made plans with Teddy this evening. You know how disappointed he can get when you leave him high and dry," Fanny interrupted. Becky gave her a sideways glance that fired more daggers than a Tommy gun did bullets.

"Is Teddy your beau?" Herbert asked with a raised chin.

"Now, why would my mama invite you for lunch to meet me if I had a beau? Teddy is not my beau. He's my neighbor since we were kids, and he knows all about you paying me a visit this afternoon. Fanny, don't you have something else you could be doing?" Becky snapped.

Fanny flipped her hair but didn't budge and instead focused on straightening the seams in her stockings. Herbert focused on Becky, much to Becky's surprise.

"I'll be back to pick you up around five, Rebecca. Oh, and wear your best dress because I'm going to parade you around town like the prettiest float in a Fourth of July parade," Herbert said as he stood up. Although he was an alderman, full in the gut and chest, he dressed snappily and smelled like cool cotton sheets.

"So you don't want any lunch?" Becky asked, a little surprised at her own disappointment that Herbert was going to leave right away.

He looked as if he'd forgotten all about it. "Hey,

can you give it to me on the run? I've got to get my suit pressed and my Flivver polished."

Becky stood up and went to go in the kitchen when she was struck with a better idea. "Fanny, be a dear and go tell Lucy to wrap up a few sandwiches for Mr. Coleman to take with him. Thanks," Becky said as she smoothed the front of her dress.

Fanny lowered her chin and glared at her cousin for a second. Herbert had his back to Fanny, so he didn't notice the swish of her hips and the flounce of her dress as she swaggered out of the room.

"Okay, she's gone. You can come clean now," Becky said in a soft voice. "You seemed very interested in my cousin last night. I know she must have given you the cold shoulder. This is just a way to give her her comeuppance, right?"

Herbert stood there for a second then smiled. "You know your cousin can't dance."

"You ain't just whistling Dixie," Becky tittered. It was a well-known fact that Fanny had two left feet. There were many bruised and battered toes to prove it.

"Let me just say it don't mean a thing if you ain't got that swing." Herbert clicked his tongue and winked. Becky held his gaze and smiled. There was something very charming about Herbert Coleman.

She liked him. It wasn't love. But she had to admit that for the first time since her mother started fixing her up, she was looking forward to seeing him later.

"What do you mean, he's leaving?" Kitty could be heard in the kitchen. Within seconds she was through the kitchen door, down the hallway, and in her sitting room, holding a sack filled with what was supposed to be a sit-down lunch on the porch.

"My goodness, Mr. Coleman, you aren't leaving yet, are you? What has she done? Did she say something to put you off?" Kitty asked nervously.

"Mother!" Becky huffed.

"Ha! On the contrary, Mrs. MacKenzie. I do appreciate your hospitality. But as I told Miss Rebecca, I'll be back to show her a good time this evening. I've got tickets to the main event. Is that for me?" Herbert asked, eyeing the sack Kitty was holding. Kitty smiled, stepped forward, and handed the food over. Herbert peeked inside then looked up, seeming quite satisfied with the contents.

"Herbert, let me walk you to your car," Becky said as she slipped her hand through the crook of his arm. She could feel the shock in her mother's expression as she escorted her date out the front door. Becky and Herbert exchanged a few more pleasantries on the porch before the sound of his engine chugging to life and driving off was all that was left of their meeting. When Becky walked back into the house, she intentionally headed for her room.

"Rebecca! Where do you think you're going, young lady?" Kitty stood there with a grin a mile wide and her hands on her hips.

"Oh, Mama. You're not going to give me the third degree?" Becky teased.

"You get back here and sit down. I want to know what it is about this Herbert Coleman that brought such a beautiful smile to my daughter's face," Kitty said and took a seat in her favorite chair.

"Mama, there isn't anything special about Herbert Coleman. He's just a regular gent. I've never been to a boxing match. I thought it sounded like fun. Please don't call the justice of the peace. Mr. Coleman will have ample time to disappoint, I assure you," Becky teased.

"I think he's rather jingle-brained," Fanny offered as she walked into the parlor.

"Horsefeathers," Becky snapped. "You're just mad because he gave you the bum's rush."

"He was at the club last night, Aunt Kitty. I think he's quite the lounge lizard. There wasn't a girl there he didn't try necking." Fanny folded her arms and raised her chin.

"That's not true." Becky rolled her eyes. "He didn't try necking on me."

"Of course, he didn't try on you. You had a sour disposition," Fanny replied.

"I'm going upstairs. Mama, do you mind if I have lunch alone in my room? I've got to decide what I'm going to wear tonight. Herbert said to wear my best dress." Becky narrowed her eyes at her cousin while she spoke.

"Yes, dear. I'd suggest your blue dress with the peacock feathers. It looks so lovely with your red hair," Kitty bubbled, completely ignoring Fanny's frown.

CHAPTER 4

*A*t five o'clock sharp, Herbert Coleman arrived in a freshly polished Flivver, his hair slicked tightly in place, and wearing a pinstriped double-breasted suit set off with a white carnation in the lapel. When Becky appeared in the blue dress her mother had suggested, the one with the hem of iridescent peacock feathers, she heard his breath hitch.

"Why Miss Rebecca, you are the cat's pajamas," Herbert said and offered his arm.

"You're looking quite dapper yourself," she said.

Within minutes, Herbert was speeding down the dirt road that led to the MacKenzie home. Becky felt the wind in her face, smelled the musky scent of the tobacco leaves, and felt happy and excited.

"Your mama told me you were on the mend after a breakup," Herbert shouted over the engine.

"What?" Becky barked and put her hands up to her cheeks. "She's a real number, that one is! When did she spill the beans?"

"I must tell you she told me immediately. I'd barely gotten my name out of my mouth, and she was singing like a canary all about it. I must say, Miss Rebecca, that your previous love must have been off his rocker to let you slip away."

"You barely know me, Herbert," Becky shouted over the engine.

"I've got a gut feeling. I didn't get where I am by being a maroon." He lifted his chin and slicked his hair back on the side with his left hand while still steering with the right. A lot of good it did, since they were all over the road, much like when Becky drove.

It took no time at all to arrive at the Silver Club, where Herbert had made reservations. Becky was impressed. Everything in the joint looked polished, like Herbert. The waiters buzzed from table to table in smooth steps like they were choreographed. The band at the front of the room played in front of panels with the initials SC scrolled across them. Many of the ladies looked like they were a good bit younger than their dates, who ordered bottles of champagne like it was as cheap as corn whiskey. Diamonds on bracelets and pinky rings sparked almost as brightly as the light off the chandeliers.

"This is a clubhouse for heavies," Becky whispered. "There could be a raid any minute."

"Not in this joint. Come on, let's get our table. I'm starved. I hope you're hungry," Herbert said as he stretched his arm out for Becky to walk ahead of him. All eyes were on her as she followed the maître d' to their table. It was a high-backed velvet booth that allowed for them to survey the entire room.

Becky slid behind the table and was thrilled when Herbert ordered two champagne cocktails. They had a round and then another. When the food came, Becky was famished, since every story Herbert told was funnier than the last. She'd not laughed so hard in so long she didn't dare try to remember.

"I've got to tell you, Herbert. I was ready to hand you your walking papers this afternoon when you showed up. The last thing a girl wants is to be someone's *second* choice," she said before taking another bite of steak.

"I've got a confession to make, Rebecca. I knew exactly who you were and that Fanny was your cousin," Herbert said, staring straight at her with a serious look on his face.

Becky didn't know if she should be angry, flattered, neither, or both. "Why didn't you introduce yourself last night? Why would you go to Fanny if you knew who I was? And why did you act so surprised this afternoon? That sort of shock is hard to fake."

"I'm not trying to toot my own horn, but a guy like me has to be careful of the people he associates with. I told you I was no maroon. I don't pack the lead like a lot of these guys do, but I do want to protect my investments. So, I knew you had a cousin who everyone said was a real looker," Herbert started.

"Who's everyone?" Becky asked but didn't really care about the answer.

"I wanted to see what your response would be if I asked her to dance. There are plenty of dames who would have told me to stay away, to be careful of all the holes from gold digging. But you didn't. You handled it with class. That's what a man needs. A broad with class."

Becky wasn't a sucker for flattery. But when it came to her cousin, she would take it.

"Let me guess. Fanny gets a lot of the cream, doesn't she?" Herbert added.

"Look, that is true," Becky said. "And I did get the brush-off from my main squeeze, and it's left me a little raw. But I'm not looking for charity or wedding bells. I'm looking to have a good time tonight. That's as far ahead I want to make plans, Herbert. I hope I'm not being a wet blanket."

"Not at all, doll. I think we've got time for one more cocktail before we blow. You'll love the fights, honey. Have you ever been?"

"No. But I've always wanted to. For no other reason than there's so much talk about them these days. I've seen Jack Dempsey and Tommy Loughran's names in the papers. But I wouldn't know either one of them if they came up and bit me." Becky giggled as she sipped the last of her drink.

"Well, these pugs aren't nearly that glamorous. But sometimes that makes for a better time, when you don't know what to expect," Herbert said before waving the waiter over and getting two more drinks and the check. Becky turned her head as he paid the bill but heard him peel off several bills from a roll he'd had in his pocket. She didn't care if a cat had lettuce or not. Adam never had much more than two nickels to rub together, and she always had a time with him. But she had to admit that it was nice to have a man who didn't have to pinch his pennies.

Once they'd finished their drinks, they headed to the Hostess City Gym on the outskirts of downtown Savanah. The place was jumping with people and cars going every which way, and the crowd of people filing in the double doors ranged from top drawer to skid row and everywhere in between. Becky's eyes boggled.

"Come on, doll. Let's make an appearance," Herbert said as he pulled up to the joint and handed his keys to a kid who was no taller than a fire hydrant. "If I get it back without a scratch, there's a sawbuck in it for you."

"Yessir," the boy replied before hopping in behind the wheel. Herbert hurried to Becky's door, opened it, and offered her his hand. She took it, noticing how soft it was and wondered if he'd ever done anything harder than make reservations. It was a complete contrast to Adam's rough mitts. Everything about him was. But that was half of what made him so charming. As interested as she was in seeing this fight, she still wasn't a hundred percent sold on Herbert Coleman. Although his opinion of Fanny did sweeten the pot.

As they entered the arena, there was a fight already in progress. The air was hazy with cigar smoke. People were shouting and cheering for the pugs to knock each other's blocks off. The smell of peanuts and popcorn was intoxicating even after Becky had had a full meal. She held on to Herbert's arm as he wove through the crowd to their seats.

"This is our spot?" she gasped as she looked at the ring. They were so close she could see the blood on the canvas from the previous bout and was sure she'd gotten a few drops of sweat thrown in her direction from the two contenders currently duking it out.

"This is it, baby. How about some peanuts?"

"I'd love some," she squealed. They took their seats, and the excitement of the room was as contagious as a cold. Within minutes, Becky was cheering with the rest of the crowd. She didn't know who was winning, and she didn't care. It was thrilling. Herbert pulled a thick cigar from his breast pocket and lit up. Becky thought it suited him. They talked and told stories, and there wasn't time for Becky to even think of Adam in between the peanuts and the fights and the people around them.

"The guy in the black shorts got the bulge on the

other. This won't go two more rounds," Herbert said through his teeth, which held his cigar.

"I don't know. I think the guy in the red shorts is holding back. You care to make a wager?" Becky shouted over the noise of the crowd.

"Why, Rebecca, I had no idea you were the gambling type. I'll bet you a dime that Black Trunks knocks out Red Trunks within the next two rounds," Herbert said as he pulled out a shiny new dime.

"You've got yourself a deal. And please stop calling me Rebecca. My friends call me Becky," she said, unable to control her smile.

"Well, Becky, I look forward to being a dime richer." Herbert winked as the bell rang and both fighters went to their respective corners for some ice on their guts and towels across their bloodied faces.

Becky was leaning forward in her seat as she looked around the arena. The people next to her were pleasant folks jabbering to one another and anyone else who would listen. She cracked a peanut shell and popped the peanut in her mouth as she looked down the row. At the end was a man who looked like the man who had come up to her in Willie's just the night before. His clothes were dirty and worn thin at the knees and elbows. His hair was disheveled, and he was slouching over almost to the point of falling out of the chair. It was like no one seemed to notice him except Becky. This was no place to be taking a nap. As if he'd read her thoughts, the man's eyes snapped open and instantly found hers. He grinned and pointed.

"They know you're here!" he shouted.

Becky straightened as goose bumps raced over her arms and across the top of her shoulders. How could this be the same guy? Was he following her? How could he be? Herbert had picked her up at her house and drove like a Keystone Cop all the way downtown. There was no way anyone like him could have kept up.

"It won't be long now!" he shouted. Everyone in the seats around her looked from the bum to Becky and back. Herbert didn't seem to notice, being too engrossed in the fight that was just a few feet from them.

Swallowing hard, Becky looked for help from someone, but they seemed as shocked as she was. How did this transient get a seat this close to the ring? How did he know Becky was there? He'd all but attacked her at Willie's. What was he going to do next? Slowly the man started to get up. A fellow in a yellow suit with wide dark-blue pinstripes and a bowler stood up and put his hand on the man's dirty lapel.

"Look, pal. You got a beef, take it outside. No one wants any trouble," Bowler said. He was joined by a couple of Brunos all too eager and juiced up not to step in. Becky was sure that bum would never get past them. But he punched the man in the bowler, laying him out flat in the lap of his date, who started screaming.

All eyes focused on the brouhaha outside the ring. Even Herbert was pulled away from the two pugs duking it out and looked past Becky to see the bum wrestling with two other guys.

"No!" Becky screamed. Her eyes bugged as she pointed down the row.

"What is it, Becky?" Herbert asked. "They're just having a row. Don't worry about it."

"No! I've seen that man before. He tried to grab me last night. Right after you asked about Fanny. He was there! Now he's here?"

"What?" Herbert puffed out his chest, slipped one arm around Becky's waist, and in one swift movement picked her up and swung her around, putting himself between her and the hobo. With both fists raised, he stepped up and pulled back, and as the crazy man set his sights on Herbert, he was hit square in the kisser. Down he went like a sack of potatoes.

Becky gasped, both hands coming up to cover her gaping mouth. She felt overwhelmed and was afraid she was about to faint. Quickly she took her seat and lowered her head. It was unbearably hot, and the smells of cigars and popcorn were starting to make her feel green in the gills. If she didn't get a hold of herself, she was going to make an even bigger scene than she already had.

"Becky? Becky, what's the matter?" Herbert asked, his face full of worry.

"It's nothing. I think I've had one too many," she replied, even though she was as sober as a one-man funeral.

"You look like someone stepped on your grave. Let's get you some fresh air. It'll help you get your legs back," Herbert said, offering her his thick, meaty paw that had red knuckles from where he'd socked the bum.

"Fresh air sounds good." Becky nodded as she took his hand. Herbert held her around her waist, not loosely. But she could tell he was no masher. Once they were outside, the fresh air, even though it was still heavy and warm, was better than what she'd been in.

"I'm sorry, Herbert. I don't know who that man is."

"Well, he'll find himself behind the eight ball if he thinks about messing with Rebecca MacKenzie while Herbert Coleman is around." He smirked. "Come on, tomato. Let's scram. I've had enough, too, and I hate losing my money," Herbert said as he handed Becky that shiny dime. She didn't even realize that the pug in the red trunks had not only lasted the two rounds but had knocked out his opponent with a one-two sock in the kisser.

"Oh, I hadn't even realized… Let's just say I saw one knockout, and it wasn't in the ring." Becky chuckled. "Did you hurt your hand?"

"Are you kidding? I've gotten in my fair number of scrapes. I don't even notice the sting anymore. Plus, no one has been able to mess up this beautiful face," he said, jutting out his chin. Becky laughed. "So, what do you say to a nightcap, kitten? We can go somewhere close to home. How about Willie's?"

Becky thought for a moment about a quick drink and maybe a dance, but it was obvious she had had enough. Her dress was starting to feel uncomfortable, her right shoe was pinching, and when she couldn't stop the yawn that stretched her mouth open, she had to decline.

"I'm sorry, Herbert, but I think we should call it a night. I'm beat."

"All right, doll. I'll take you home," he replied with a hint of disappointment in his voice. As they drove home, Herbert, using both lanes of traffic, chatted enthusiastically about his work and how exciting the world of metalworking was. Becky let him talk. Although he did make the idea of making bedframes for prisons sound exciting, she couldn't shake the fact that that same hobo had gone after her not just once but twice.

When they pulled up to her house, Herbert walked her to the door. He promised to come back the following day to check on her.

"That would be lovely," Becky said and really meant it.

"Good," Herbert said and shook her hand politely. He left in a cloud of dust. Becky went in through the front door. The house was quiet, and she was glad for it. Bed. That was all that was on her mind. After stripping out of her clothes and shimmying into her nightgown, Becky turned out the lamp on her nightstand, slipped under just the sheet, and was happy sleep came quickly. However, she didn't rest.

CHAPTER 5

*B*ecky heard her mother's voice and felt her hands on her shoulders shaking her before she realized what was happening.

"Becky, you're having a bad dream. Wake up, sweetheart!" Kitty's voice was firm, but Becky heard the concern in it and responded with blinking her eyes open.

"What? What's going on?" Becky snapped to before rubbing her eyes. She looked around and was surprised to see Lucretia was also standing in her room, holding her tray of coffee and two biscuits.

"You were screaming bloody murder. That's what's going on," Kitty said as she smoothed Becky's hair down. Becky sank back into her pillow and squinted a moment. As hard as she tried to sift through the fog in her head, she couldn't grasp what she'd dreamt about.

"I don't know, Mama. I can't remember a thing." She swallowed and tugged her sheet up to her chin. "Maybe I swallowed a bad batch of giggle juice?"

"Oh, you really are impossible." Kitty tickled Becky under the chin as she'd done often when her daughter was little and reluctant to get out of bed for her school lessons. It still had the same effect and made Becky laugh.

"Would you like your coffee, Miss Becky?" Lucretia asked, chuckling as well.

"Yes, Lucy. Thanks," Becky replied and scooted herself into a sitting position.

"How was your date last night?" Kitty asked. "I heard Mr. Coleman took you to the Silver Club. Your father and I have only been there twice, and it was for a very special occasion, not just a date. Herbert must think very highly of you."

Becky shrugged as Lucretia placed her breakfast tray on her lap. Within a matter of seconds, she'd buttered her biscuit and had shoved half of it in her mouth.

"It wasn't bad," Becky said with her mouth full.

"Wasn't bad? Why, that young man showed you off in the most expensive restaurant in town, and all you can say is it wasn't bad? Oh, Rebecca, I've got half a mind to call him on the phone this instant and tell him to forget courting you. Did I raise my only child to be so ungrateful?" Kitty said as she pushed herself off the bed and brushed off her skirt.

"Would you?" Becky teased back, making Lucretia titter as she left the room.

"Rebecca Madeline, what am I going to do with you?" Kitty looked flustered, and although there was nothing Becky liked more than to tease her mama mercilessly, she didn't like to see her upset.

"Oh, Mama. I'm just yanking your chain. I must admit… that… Herbert… was a real bacon-and-eggs man," Becky admitted.

"Becky, I have no idea what in the world that means. Can you speak the King's English?" Kitty sighed.

"He was a real gentleman, and I had a very nice time. In fact—" Becky took a deep breath and looked at her mother before rolling her eyes. "I wouldn't mind seeing him again."

"Really?" Kitty asked softly, her hand at her throat.

"Please, Mama, don't call all those old biddies of yours and tell them the wedding is in the spring. I'm just saying that we get along and had a nice time."

"And that you wouldn't mind seeing him again," Kitty repeated, making Becky sorry she'd said anything.

"Promise me you won't be spreading this around town," Becky pleaded.

"I won't say a word. My lips are sealed," Kitty said. "Finish your breakfast then come downstairs. We've got errands to run today."

Becky nodded and took another bite. She saw the sly look on her mother's face and was sure she was going to be gossiping relentlessly to her father, Lucretia, and Moxley, and if Fanny got wind of it, the whole town of Savannah would be hearing about it minus any facts or truth.

"Oh, Mama! I remember what I dreamt about. It was horrible! Horrible!"

"What, child? What could have scared you that badly?"

"I dreamt that... Cousin Fanny was moving in... permanently. She was never going to leave. Never ever! It was horrible!" Becky bit her knuckle as she looked at her mother. Kitty was not laughing or even slightly amused. She shook her head and left the room.

Becky finished her breakfast and quickly got dressed. If she did have a nightmare, she didn't remember a shred of it. How bad could it have been?

You were screaming bloody murder, Kitty had said. Becky thought for a moment and wondered what it could have been all about. She did have a lovely time with Herbert. She got home rather early but couldn't remember why that was. In fact, there was a good chunk of the night she couldn't recall. Suddenly she wasn't feeling all that great. Like she was being watched. She looked around her room. Nothing was out of place. When she glanced out the window, there was no one peeping in. Just to make sure, she walked over and leaned out, looking left and right. There wasn't a soul about. Still, she couldn't shake that feeling. She pulled her curtains closed and finished bustling about before going downstairs. But the feeling followed her. As she went into the dining room, she saw that her father was there.

"Good morning, Daddy," she said to the man behind the newspaper.

"Good morning. Your mother says you..."

"We're not getting married or even going steady. Herbert and I *might* have another date. That's as far as it goes," Becky huffed as she flopped in her seat.

"I was going to say your mother said you had a nightmare. I was sure the date had gone south when

I heard that," Judge MacKenzie said, looking at his daughter from around the paper. He always wore a smart suit, even if he was going out into the tobacco fields. But he was not afraid to get his shoes and hands dirty if there was work that needed to be done. That was why his workers loved him almost as much as Becky did.

"Oh, that. Yeah. I dreamt Fanny was staying with us permanently," Becky replied without emotion as she pulled out her chair and sat to her father's right.

"That would do it to me too," he said softly before giving Becky a wink. "Speak of the devil."

Just then, Fanny came sashaying into the dining room. It was obvious from her outfit that Kitty had already informed her that a trip downtown was necessary today. Not to be outdone by her country-bumpkin cousin, Fanny had put on a smart plaid dress that dipped dangerously low in the front and held tightly around the waist.

"*Bonjour*," she chirped before taking a seat.

"Morning, Fanny. You're looking mighty pretty today," Judge replied without looking up.

"Aunt Kitty said we were going downtown, so I thought I'd clean myself up a bit. You missed all the excitement last night, Becky. It's a shame you didn't join Herbert for a nightcap at Willie's," Fanny said, peering over her cup as she sipped her coffee.

"What?" Becky asked.

"He showed up there after dropping you off. He said you weren't feeling well and didn't want a nightcap but that he still thought there was a lot of night left. So he stopped off." Fanny smoothed her hair.

"That's true," Becky replied with a shrug.

"You weren't feeling well?" Judge asked.

"It's nothing, Daddy. I was just out of sorts. A sip of bad hooch is all, I'm sure. I'm fine now." She patted her father's hand, and he replied with a satisfied nod before going back to his paper.

"Well, Mr. Coleman certainly didn't let any moss grow on him. I think he danced with half the dames in the place. Some of them were on the prowl too," Fanny said with her chin raised, looking down at Becky.

"So what? I've danced with most of the fellas at Willie's. It just means I like to dance. Herbert told me he did too. He was just out after a... strange night and letting off a little steam. Besides, Fanny, not that it's any of your business, but I don't have any ties on Mr. Coleman any more than *you* do."

Fanny shrugged. "I just thought you should know

that he doesn't let his size inhibit him from getting the attention of the ladies."

"What's the matter, Fanny? Are you mad that he's spreading himself thin or that he's not tripping and falling all over you? You just have to admit that you blew your chances with the guy because he wasn't some big, rod-carrying roscoe with just enough brain cells to dress himself every day."

"You really do have the manners of a field hen," Fanny replied.

"At least I have some kind of manners," Becky needled.

"You don't deserve a man like Herbert Coleman. He's much too classy and just a decent fellow. I never realized how sensitive he was until we talked last night. We talked and talked, and you are out of your league, Rebecca. I'm sorry to say it, but you are." Fanny placed her napkin on her lap and reached for the plate of biscuits on the table.

"That's enough, Fanny," Judge interrupted.

"It's all right, Daddy. Everyone knows Fanny thinks she's better than us. Maybe she is. We were the only relatives who disregarded reputation to take such a scandalous Sheba in." Becky returned the insult and then some. It had the desired effect. Fanny gasped. Her cheeks lit up, and she glared at Becky, who helped herself to another biscuit.

"That's enough out of both of you. Now, if you two gals can't learn to get along at the table, then one of you will be eating out in the shed. I don't care which one. Understand me? I look forward to reading the Savannah news before I get out on the plantation. It calms me. The last things I want to hear are the petty grievances of the women in this house," Judge said, making both ladies look down at their hands.

"What's going on in here?" Kitty asked then pinched her lips together when no one spoke. "Rebecca, are you two nitpicking again?"

"She started it." Becky pointed at Fanny.

"You started it. I was making pleasantries, and you went off on a bender that Mr. Coleman wasn't interested in me or anyone else and…" Fanny bit her lip when Kitty put her hand on her shoulder.

"Did Mr. Coleman tell you he was interested in you?" Kitty asked nervously. If the man she'd fixed her daughter up with turned out to be indecent, Kitty would be mortified.

"Well, no," Fanny replied, making Becky smirk and fold her arms in front of her. "I was just saying how he danced with quite a number of girls, not all of them from respectable families." Fanny folded her arms across her chest.

"I've heard enough of all of it," Judge interrupted as he pushed himself from the table. "You girls need to work out your differences before you all come to the table. I will not tolerate this kind of behavior under my roof," Judge said before kissing Kitty on the cheek. "Teach these girls to be proper ladies, Mama. Use my belt if you have to."

Becky smirked at her dad, who winked at her and rolled his eyes behind Fanny's back.

"I may do just that. Rebecca, if you don't stop antagonizing your cousin, I'm going to... to..." Kitty folded her arms. "Well, I'll think of something, and it might just include your father's belt."

Becky looked at her mother with pinched lips. It never failed that Fanny escaped criticism while Becky took the brunt of her mother's scolding. Someday she was going to remind her mother of all these injustices and demand retribution. But it was no use trying to win this battle today. She had other things to worry about, like the blank spot in her memory.

"Where do we have to go today?" Becky asked as they piled in her father's Flivver with Moxley at the wheel. Kitty sat in the front while Becky shared the back seat with Fanny. She had the feeling there would be a lot of waiting and yawning, so she brought her sketchbook and pencils with her. Kitty's answer to her question made her thankful she brought her own entertainment.

"Well, I saw there was a sale on dresses at Gimbels, and I was hoping to find something a little less showy for the Potts' end-of-the-summer party. You know, the whole town will be there, and it's always such an exquisite affair. You had a wonderful time last year. Do you remember, Becky?" Kitty asked. The memory had brought a smile to her mama's face, so Becky played along.

"Oh, yes. They had that new croquet set, and we played hide-and-seek when the sun went down," Becky replied. The truth was she'd had a horrible time, since they played old-timer music that was impossible to dance to, and during the game of hide-and-seek, Becky managed to hide herself in a patch of poison ivy. She itched for days.

"That's right. So I want you girls to look for dresses too," Kitty said proudly.

"Oh goody!" Fanny exclaimed. "I was thinking that I needed a lime-green colored dress. It would bring out the green flecks in my eyes. They are usually quite blue, but in the right light with the right complementary colors, they can be slightly green. When I was in Paris, I was told by Madame Monet that my eyes were the most unusual, for they seemed to shift from color to color."

Becky bit her tongue. She didn't want to ruin her mother's good intentions. But the last thing she wanted to do was shop for another dress. It was boring.

"Mama, Gimbels is not far from a little shop on Bryn Mawr Street that I like to go to," Becky said. "Would you mind if I stopped there for a spell and caught up with you later? I promise I won't be long."

"I don't see why not, dear. What is the shop?" Kitty asked. "Maybe we'd all like to go."

"Oh, I don't think you'd like it. It's an apothecary, and they sell sketchbooks you can get on the cheap," Becky replied. If she told her mother the truth about this specific apothecary, she was sure that Kitty just might faint.

"Well, do hurry. I'd like to be able to see you try on a couple of dresses," Kitty replied.

"I will. I promise," Becky said.

Moxley knew where Becky was going. He'd taken her there and picked her up dozens of times and kept her secret. He was a good egg that way.

"I'll be back down in a jiffy, Moxley," Becky said.

He'd dropped off Kitty and Fanny at Gimbels first.

"Take your time, Miss Becky. I'm going to stop for a shine and a cigar. I'll meet you back at the car."

Becky nodded and hurried into the shop. The door jingled. Instantly Becky spotted Ophelia, who had actually been smiling pleasantly at an older couple standing at the counter. Ophelia looked at her with her one good eye as the other, white with cataracts, seemed to see something else. She gave her a slight smirk. That was as good as a how-do-you-do and a clap on the back from Ophelia.

"Well, look who it is," Ophelia grumbled. Since the day they met, the old woman had treated Becky like an annoying hair on her chin that continued to grow back after multiple pluckings. Not that Ophelia seemed at all interested in plucking the hairs on her chin.

The old couple turned and looked at Becky, who smiled politely. "Is Cecelia upstairs?" she asked. Madame Cecelia was Becky's dear friend. Only Martha took precedence over the exotic woman who knew all about Becky's powers and helped her to not only stop fearing them but embrace them.

"She is. What do you want?"

"I want to talk to her. You know, chew the fat for a while," Becky replied, her eyebrows arching innocently, like a child asking permission for her friend to come out and play.

"Excuse me, young lady, but that is a beautiful brooch you are wearing," the old woman at the counter interrupted, pointing a chubby, wrinkled hand at Becky, who looked down at her lapel. She'd forgotten she'd adorned it with a midnight-blue peacock brooch.

"Thank you," Becky replied politely before looking back at Ophelia as if waiting for her to say something. The old woman, who was not as schooled in manners as Becky, shook her head before pinching her lips together like the words about to come out tasted sour.

"These are the Veros. They moved in next door," Ophelia remarked.

Becky, who had been raised to introduce herself and make people feel welcome since the day she first learned how to speak confidently, walked up to the couple and extended her hand.

"That's swell. Welcome to Savannah. I don't think you could ask for better neighbors," Becky replied, swallowing hard as she looked at Ophelia, who rolled her eyes.

"Thank you, young lady. We were so glad to find out that our neighbors were from our country too.

It's like having a piece of home here with us," Mrs. Vero said in very good English. She had a round face in contrast to Ophelia's long, chiseled mug. It didn't look like Mrs. Vero or her husband had missed many meals. Both were plump around the middle, and their clothes were old in style. Still, Becky could tell they were well made without a tatter anywhere to be found, nor a spot of any kind.

Mr. Vero looked strong for a man his age. His wrists dangled well past the cuff of his coat, like he'd grown out of it a long time ago. His pants were the same, exposing his ankles. But that was a style everyone in Savannah had seen from the folks who came from overseas. Some people thought it was an indication that the folks were rubes. To Becky, it was charming.

"That is a blessing, isn't it?" Becky replied. "Why, I grew up living next door to my very best friend, Teddy, who is just berries. I couldn't tell you how many scrapes he's gotten me out of that..." Becky swallowed after she looked at Ophelia and took the hint. The look on her face was more annoyed than usual. "Ophelia, you look different to me today. Have you done something new to your hair? Whatever it is, it's swell. The bee's knees, really."

"Cecelia's upstairs." Ophelia, who was Cecelia's

mother, jerked her thumb over her shoulder toward the stairs. The old woman was not an easy nut to crack. "But I don't like what you are bringing up there with you."

"What am I bringing up with me?" Becky asked. All Ophelia did was shake her head. It was that white eye. It could see things her normal eye didn't. A blessing and a curse. Becky could never hide anything from Ophelia. Maybe that was why the old woman spooked her a little. Or maybe it was because she was a tough old broad. Actually, Becky couldn't say she was completely afraid of Ophelia. It wasn't fear. It was respect. The old woman demanded it with every glance or comment. And why shouldn't she? She came to America like so many other immigrants and set up a home and shop and was making a living. That was what America was built on. But, like Becky, she had gifts, talents that scared most people. Becky wondered if sometimes Ophelia didn't get spooked by her own abilities. Now wasn't the time to ask her.

"It was a pleasure meeting you," Becky said to the Veros, who both nodded.

With one last glimpse at Ophelia, Becky slinked behind the counter and up the stairs without another word.

Before she could knock on the door, she heard a loud cry. "Come in! Where have you been?"

Becky stepped into the apartment that was over the apothecary and smiled as soon as she saw Cecelia. The woman towered over Becky and had one of those hourglass figures that only a man who stood six-foot-four could handle. Her hair was jet-black and piled high on her head in a bun. Her lips and nails were always red, and no matter what she wore, she couldn't hide her feminine assets. Even in the plain brown skirt and black blouse she was wearing today, she'd turn every head in Savannah if she ventured outside.

"You know me, Cecelia. Not in any place too long," Becky replied before giving her friend a tight hug.

"You're doing better, then? Your heart isn't so broken anymore?" Cecelia knew all about Adam and the breakup of the century.

"It's still broken, but I'm doing better," Becky replied. She could have started to cry. It was how she always felt when she spoke about Adam. But she didn't and instead smiled.

"Good. Let's not talk about him. Let's talk about this new man," Cecelia said with a wink.

CHAPTER 6

here was something exceptionally cozy about Cecelia's apartment. It was cluttered with trinkets and pictures of exotic-looking faces and places. There were lush green plants hanging from the ceiling by the fire escape, which also was home to some thriving plants. However, it had been so hot and muggy for the past several days, it was only the churn of an old fan that stirred the air. Becky was sweating, but when Cecelia brought her a glistening glass of lemonade, she instantly felt better.

"How do you know I was out with a new man?" Becky asked, already sure she knew the answer.

Unlike most people who were gifted with perfect

hindsight, Cecelia was gifted with that and an uncanny ability to see the future. Not all of it or every detail. But she knew of Becky's date before Becky knew she would be going on one.

"Darling, please. Let's not waste time with silly questions," Cecelia teased. "This was a man your mother had found for you?"

"Yes. She means well, and I have been mopey these past couple of weeks. I don't want to talk about him, Cecelia, but I miss Adam. Although not as much today." Becky raised her eyebrows as she took a sip of lemonade.

"What did you and this man do on your date?" Cecelia asked as she sat down across from Becky, a deck of tarot cards in her hands. She began to shuffle them casually.

"Well, that's the rub, see," Becky started. She told of their dinner and the conversation and described Mr. Herbert Coleman to a tee. "But for the life of me, I can't remember anything else. Something had to have happened. He brought me home early because I didn't want a nightcap. Me! Not wanting a nightcap? It's like I started the date and someone else stepped in to ruin the rest. I just can't remember a thing until I got home."

Cecelia set her cards down and reached for

Becky's sketchbook. Without saying anything, she opened the book and began to admire Becky's drawings.

"You have a real talent, Miss Becky. These are very good. I think we can figure out what happened to you," Cecelia said as she flipped past the drawings to an empty page.

"What do you mean?"

"You are going to draw it. It is an old tactic that my mother is familiar with," Cecelia said.

"Will it make me blind in one eye?" Becky asked, only half joking.

Cecelia chuckled. "No. But it might make you as fitsy as a polecat," Cecelia replied, making them both chuckle. "I want you to take up your pencil and close your eyes. Imagine a quiet place where you can rest. You are there. It is peaceful."

Becky listened to Cecelia's voice, and in an instant, she was in the Old Brick Cemetery under her favorite shade tree. It was always calm, quiet, and safe there. No one liked to go into the old bone-yard, too full of superstitions and fearful of the souls roaming about. But Becky had always felt at home there. Becky could hear Cecelia's voice, which sounded like a soft wind rustling the trees.

"Let your mind connect with your hand holding

your pencil. Draw what you are seeing there. A small thing or a grand thing. Pretty or ugly. Let your mind look at it while your hand creates," Cecelia instructed.

Becky could feel her hand moving, but she didn't see her drawing emerging from the page. Instead, she only saw what she was looking at. The cracked and weather-worn fence of the cemetery that was more weeds than anything else.

"Now, while you are in this safe and peaceful place, show me your new beau. What does he look like? How does he dress? Does he smile a lot, or is he serious?"

Becky felt her hand fly across the page as the image of Herbert began to take shape. The feeling was like she was tracing his face with her fingers and feeling the fabric of his suit. Then, the words that changed everything were spoken.

"Miss Becky, what did you do last night?" It wasn't like Cecelia was accusing Becky of anything. The words hit her ears like she was asking if she knew what the weather was going to be like. But they seized Becky's chest, and her hand began to fly across the page. She saw the boxing ring. She saw the man at the end of the row, who was the same man who had grabbed her at Willie's. The entire incident was being replayed, and with her hand moving faster and faster across the page, Becky felt her breath hitch in her throat.

Surely, she was using up all the space on the paper. There would be nothing but scribbles and lines that no one would be able to differentiate from one another. It would be a swirled, convoluted mess. Still, Becky continued to scribble, unable to stop herself.

"You were at a bout. Seeing a couple of pugs go at it and..." All she saw now was a dark, dark place. The air was still heavy with humidity, even though it was pitch black outside. She was in the shadows but not hiding. She didn't need to hide. She could see what was going on. A man holding the right side of his face was staggering down what looked like the railroad tracks. Becky hadn't gone anywhere near the railroad tracks last night. Unless...

"Becky, what did you see last night?" Becky heard the words, and her hand moved in a flurry of strokes and scribbles, but she had no idea what she was drawing. She only knew that what she was seeing, she didn't like. The man holding his face was the man from the fight. He was staggering. Herbert must have really given it to him. Or he'd hit the sauce. Maybe a little of both. But then someone else appeared. Someone big with rounded shoulders who yanked the man by the collar.

"No," Becky whispered. The sound of a train coming echoed in her head. She wasn't there. This was a dream. The dream she'd had that morning.

"*You were screaming bloody murder,*" she heard her mother's voice say, but she still couldn't look away from the scene unfolding in front of her eyes. But it wasn't in front of her eyes. She didn't go to a train yard with Herbert. They left the fight. He offered to take her to Willie's, and she declined. He drove her home and was a complete gentleman. Now she remembered. But what this other scene was, she didn't know. She hadn't been there. It had been a long time since she and Martha and Teddy ventured anywhere near the train yards to a shanty or gin joint along the tracks.

"Get him on the tracks," a voice from the shadows ordered. The hunched figure did as it was told. The hobo tried to fight but was no match for the bigger, healthier man. Becky continued to draw. Her hand flew across the page. Tears began to sting her eyes as the sound of a train whistle could be heard in the distance.

"No," Becky whispered.

"You stay right there," the voice called out. It was a hoarse voice, like someone who had been singing at the top of their lungs for at least four songs.

"No," the hobo muttered.

Becky could see a gun in the shadow's hand. In a flash, he pulled the trigger. It echoed like he'd done it in a tunnel. The hobo grabbed his leg as he cried out in pain.

"He's going to attract attention!" the scratchy voice hissed. "Snuff him out!"

The hunched figure lunged at the hobo, and after pummeling him worse than Herbert had done, he left the man's old, broken body on the tracks. He was still alive. Becky could see the rise and fall of his chest. But he wasn't moving. The train whistle was getting louder. The hunched figure slinked out of the way. All Becky could see was the man, the train tracks, and the light of the train coming closer.

"No!" she cried. "Get up! The train is coming!"

"Becky, it's all right." She heard Cecelia's voice but didn't see her.

"Help me! Help me get him off the tracks!" Becky cried as her hand flew across the page. She was scribbling wildly, flipping the pages to start new.

"Becky, you are nowhere near the tracks. You are safe." Cecelia tried to break the spell.

"Help me get him off the tracks! The train is coming!" Becky cried.

Cecelia got out of her seat and took Becky by the shoulders. "Snap out of it! You're safe here! It's over!"

"The train is coming! It's coming!" Becky cried until the light of the locomotive blinded her and snapped her out of her trance. She was gasping and clutched Cecelia's hands.

"Now I remember my nightmare," Becky whimpered. She looked down at her sketchbook and felt a lump in her throat. It was a sketch of the man from Willie's and the fight. He was trying to get out from underneath the wheels of the train, but it was too late. She wiped her eyes and shook her head to get the fog out of it.

"Here. Take a drink." Cecelia handed Becky her glass of lemonade.

"What a ride," Becky exclaimed after taking a sip. She took another then sat back in her seat and looked at her sketchbook. "Would you get a load of this? Why, the gang and I haven't been to the train yard since the bulls almost caught us trying to sneak down the tracks to a shack near the river."

After taking the glass from Cecelia, Becky flipped

through the pages. With a few more gulps while flipping the pages, Becky was starting to feel more like herself. Cecelia had walked across the room. She picked up the newspaper and handed it to Becky.

"Becky, did you see the paper this morning?" Cecelia asked.

"No. I was too busy fussing with my mother and Fanny. Besides, Daddy had it first, and he was reading at the table. You don't dare take it from him before he's finished with..." She looked at the headline. Another hobo had been found on the train tracks, dead, his head cut off by the train as it rode by. There was a picture of the man, since he did have identification on him.

"Becky, you're sure you didn't read the paper this morning?" Cecelia asked.

Becky shook her head. "This is the man at Willie's and at the fight. He knew me and said some strange things. He was just pickled, right? Just a rummy who fell asleep on the train tracks. It happens all the time."

"It's been happening a lot these days," Cecelia said.

Becky swallowed hard. It *had* been happening a lot. "But what does this have to do with me? I just had a nightmare. Probably from a couple of bad oysters, or maybe the bathtub gin had too many juniper berries in it. Or maybe they were a bad batch. That could cause me to have an ing-bing. Heck, Teddy once had a fit after swallowing an olive whole. It gave him the flop sweats, and he swore off olives for the good part of a month."

But these were just excuses, and Becky knew there was more to it. She looked at Cecelia, who finally took her seat again across the table. She reached out her hand for the sketchbook. Becky reluctantly handed it over. She didn't want to let her see it anymore. It was so gruesome and terrible she was embarrassed to claim it.

"This is called automatic drawing," Cecelia said as she slowly flipped through the pages. "You slipped into a trance, induced by me, and were able to tap into the part of your mind that had been concealed."

"I just wanted to recall what I'd done last night. I didn't do this. I didn't go to the train yard. Herbert took me to dinner and to a boxing match, and there..." Becky let out a deep breath. She explained the confrontation with the hobo and that she'd seen him before.

"He kept saying they knew where I was. But he must have been talking off his nut because the only crazy in the joint was him. It turned into a bigger brawl than the pugs in the ring were having. Half a dozen guys tried to make the guy dummy up. Herbert finally walked over and gave him a sock in the chops, sending him down for a count to ten," Becky said. "We didn't stay. I wanted to go home. I'd had enough. So Herbert drove me home, and we made plans to get together again. That was it. I went to bed and woke up this morning to my mother shaking me awake."

When she told Cecelia that her mother said she was screaming in her sleep, Cecelia's expression became dire.

"You were there at the train yard. You were a witness to the crime, the murder of that man. But how you got linked to the killers…"

"Whoa! Sorry, Cecelia, but that sounds like a lot of hooey. I wasn't a witness to anything. I was at home in bed, and this was just a nightmare," Becky said with a huff. "I've been reading about these crazy killings, and it just got to me. Add a little too much hootch and cheap cigar smoke, and you start seeing things. It's happened before. This is nothing new."

"Becky, I'm afraid for you. Please, do me a favor. Come see me again if you have another nightmare. Please. My mother can dispel evil spirits that haunt us at night. She's very good at it,"

Cecelia said as if she were talking about her mother baking a vanilla cake and not some spiritual battle.

"I'm all right. I'll bet this is all just my mind coping with Adam leaving. Yeah, that's probably it. Can I have my sketchbook back?" Becky stood and reached out her hand. Cecelia gave the book to her. All Becky wanted to do was rush out the door, but she couldn't leave things this way.

"You're a good egg, Cecelia. We've been chummy for some time now, and I want you to know I couldn't imagine my life without you in it. But I think this was just a dream. There's no truth to it. I didn't witness anything. It was just a dream. A bad one. But I doubt I'll have any more." She looked at the clock. "I gotta blow, or I'll be in a jam with my mother for making her wait."

"My door is always open for you, Becky. You know that," Cecelia replied. Becky shuffled back, quickly gave Cecelia a tight hug, then left. As she hurried down the stairs, she ran right into Ophelia.

"Bye, Ophelia. Have a good day," Becky said as she quickly scooted past the old gray-haired witch.

"You're leaving so soon? My day is getting better," the old woman replied and cackled to herself. Becky looked at her with her eyebrows pinched together.

When Ophelia's good eye locked with Becky's, Ophelia laughed out loud.

"Always a pleasure," Becky snapped as she yanked the door open. She liked Ophelia. The old broad was feisty. But at times like this, she couldn't be sure if she was joking or really glad Becky was leaving.

Becky raced down the stairs, clutching her sketchbook and pencils as she jumped from the last two stairs in order to shave off a couple of seconds. When she burst through the door, she saw Moxley standing at the car. She hurried up to him and tossed her things in the back.

"You're going to get us in a heap of trouble, Miss Becky. We're already ten minutes late. You know how Miss Fanny works up your mother if you're the least bit delayed," he said as he held the car door open for her.

"Oh, horsefeathers. Fanny can go take a long walk off a short pier," Becky huffed.

"Did you find what you were looking for in the apothecary?" Moxley asked.

"No. Well, yes and no. I got the information I wanted, but I don't think I'll be buying what they are selling. At least not right away," Becky said. She knew she was speaking in code and that Moxley didn't know what she was really saying, but it made her feel better keeping all the gory details to herself. Heck, the last thing she wanted was for her friend to be frightened of her. Moxley would inevitably be spooked by her "talents," and she'd never be able to explain to him that they were harmless. Most people would have been spooked by her. Sometimes, like now, she spooked herself.

CHAPTER 7

*G*imbels Department Store was as active as an anthill. There were women with bags in their hands bustling back and forth, saleswomen darting here and there as they tried everything to appease these same women. Almost every inch of counter was occupied with someone demanding to see something behind the glass. Becky took a deep breath then sneezed. The smell of perfume tickled her nose.

After getting a hankie from her purse, Becky made her way through the crowd. It was inevitable that she would run into her mother's friends. A sale at Gimbels brought out all the best women in Savannah, who, in Becky's opinion, had the worst manners.

"Rebecca MacKenzie! Is that you?"

Becky wanted to shrivel up and slip through a crack in the marble floor whenever she heard her name called. She turned to see Mrs. Legare waddling in her direction. Mrs. Legare had this crazy idea that no matter how ugly a dress might be, if it was the most expensive, she wanted it. The ensemble she was wearing today was no exception. A purple dress with a dropped waist and a yellow ruffled collar made her look like some chubby exotic bird that escaped from the zoo.

"Hello, Mrs. Legare." Becky forced a smile.

"Dear, I do hope you'll be around at the end of the month. We're having a grand party for my daughter, Pauline. She's engaged, you know," Mrs. Legare said, puffing out her chest as if it might slim her belly, which was just as full.

"Oh, she is?" Becky faked interest. This was another reason she hated shopping in the department stores. If she ran into one mother whose daughter was engaged, she ran into a million. Plus, they were never marrying Harry the plumber or Paul the garbage collector. They were always marrying lawyers and doctors. Could there be a more boring group of gents? Did they all fish from the same pool?

"That's wonderful." Becky forced a smile and blinked. Mrs. Legare had to be thrilled her daughter had found a man to marry her and wasn't interested in entering her in the Kentucky Derby. Pauline had a set of choppers that would make Man o' War jealous.

"He's a doctor, you know. Has his own practice in Odell. According to town gossip, he was their most eligible bachelor for the longest time until he set eyes on my Pauline. It's just like a fairy tale."

"I'm sure. Every prince needs a trusty steed," Becky replied and stared at Mrs. Legare with a dopey smile on her face. The comment sailed past without so much as rippling the water, and Mrs. Legare just smiled.

"Yes, well, you'll come to the engagement party. As I said, it will be at the end of the month. Pauline's fiancé has loads of friends who have yet to settle down. Perhaps you'll meet someone there. Wouldn't that be lovely if you met your future husband at one of my affairs?"

"That would be ducky," Becky replied, feeling her bones trembling like they wanted to escape through her skin. "I really must find Mama, so if you'll excuse me."

"I'll tell Pauline I saw you and that you can't wait to hear all about her wedding," Mrs. Legare said.

"Mrs. Legare, if you wouldn't mind my making a suggestion," Becky said, "my cousin Fanny was invited to some of the best engagement parties in Paris. She has a real knowledge of what the upper crust is doing, and I'll bet she would love to spend the day with Pauline, hearing all about her plans. Perhaps, with the right encouragement, she would share her knowledge of the Parisian way to do an engagement party."

"That's a wonderful idea." Mrs. Legare would be like a bulldog with a bone. There was no way Fanny would get out of this. "I'll talk to Kitty. Bye-bye, now. Or should I say *au revoir*." Again, Mrs. Legare tittered as she waved her purple-gloved hand at Becky before shuffling away as fast as her chubby legs could move.

As Becky turned around to quickly get out of Mrs. Legare's range of vision, she saw her cousin making a beeline for her. Of course, her hands were full of bags and even a hat box.

"What did you do? Ask Mama to buy you the whole store?" Becky snapped.

"I'll have you know that I did protest, but Aunt Kitty insisted. The dress just wouldn't have looked right without the hat," she said, shrugging. "I'd have looked partially naked."

"Like that ever stopped you before," Becky replied.

"I'll have you know that in Paris, the gowns would be considered quite risqué for the people of Savannah. Only in some cases is fashion here starting to catch up with what is going on over there," Fanny snapped before lifting her chin.

"That's why your closet is full until bursting, because fashion here is just so run-of-the-mill. Where's Mama? I don't want her to feel she has to buy lunch on top of everything else."

"But she already said she would," Fanny pouted. "Don't you go making her feel bad for wanting to do a nice gesture. That's terribly rude and…"

"Where did you suggest we go?" Becky asked, knowing Fanny had already planted the bug in her mother's ear to take them for lunch.

"I didn't suggest anything. I just mentioned I was getting hungry, and she suggested Milton's. I can't help it if she wants to go to such a posh place." Fanny looked nervously around like she was waiting for someone to step in and tell Becky they were going to the most expensive luncheon diner in town whether she liked it or not.

"Milton's? No. I want to go to the drugstore," Becky replied. She actually loved the lunch counter.

There was nothing like getting a ham-and-cheese with a cherry soda to wash it down, and the fact that it cost only a dime made her feel better about the whole situation. Not to mention the irritation it caused her cousin.

"The drugstore?" Fanny rolled her eyes. "No. I'm not going."

"Fine. Sit in the car with Moxley. But that's what I'm telling Mama. Where is she?"

"She's in the misses department looking for dresses for you, since you can't be bothered," Fanny replied.

Becky was about to say something else, but her cousin walked away before she could get anything out of her mouth. That was probably for the best. On top of everything else, Fanny was a tattletale. Becky would have to account for herself, and the last thing she wanted to do was completely ruin her mother's attempt at getting them out together like a family.

As she made her way to the misses department, Becky spotted her mother right away. She was studying a pretty light-green dress with a dark-green trim and lovely lace across the front. As soon as she saw her daughter, Kitty held it up.

"I just knew this would go beautifully with your hair. Oh, and it makes your eyes look fiery and not just brown. Do try it on," Kitty insisted, handing the dress to Becky and pointing toward the dressing rooms.

"I will, Mama. Mama, why are you buying Fanny more clothes? She's got a closet full of things she hasn't even worn. And she's so ungrateful for it all. It drives me batty," Becky admitted.

"Rebecca, how would it look if I took my daughter shopping and bought her things but left my niece out in the cold? Do you know what people would say?"

"They'd say, look at Mrs. MacKenzie being frugal and telling that trollop *no* for a change," Becky blurted out then clapped her hand over her mouth. Her mother looked down at her with her brows pinched together.

"No. They'd say Kitty MacKenzie is cruel to only buy for her daughter when her niece has nowhere else to go. That's what they'd say," Kitty replied.

Becky felt like she was one inch tall. "All right, Mama. I won't say another word about it. But can we go to the drugstore for lunch? I just love sitting at the counter," Becky pleaded.

"On one condition. You try this dress on for the Potts' party. It would make me so happy," Kitty nudged.

"I thought Fanny was getting the green dress to bring out the green in her eyes," Becky said, batting her lashes and propping her hands underneath her chin.

"No. I wanted you in a green dress. Fanny has a pink one," Kitty said without looking at her daughter. "You are much prettier in green than she is."

"You mean, green with envy?" Becky said, exposing her insecurity to her mother.

"Why, Rebecca Madeline MacKenzie. There isn't a woman on God's green earth that can hold a candle to you. You care about people. It shows on your face. That will always make you beautiful." Kitty frowned at her daughter as if she was angry her daughter didn't know this about herself.

Becky felt a slight sting of tears in her eyes as she kissed her mother on the cheek before she slung the green dress over her shoulder and headed toward the dressing room. Before getting there, she stopped and looked at a gold velvet gown that dipped daringly low in the back. She grabbed it, too, and hurried into a vacant dressing room.

After a lot of clucking and chirping, the ladies did have lunch at the drugstore, where Fanny not only consumed a ham-and-cheese sandwich but also a hot fudge sundae with whipped cream and peanuts with a cherry on top. Becky had a slice of apple pie, and even Kitty enjoyed a scoop of peppermint ice cream.

Everyone piled in the car that Moxley had been sitting in, his cap over his nose, catching a quick catnap. As Fanny squeezed into the back seat, she picked up Becky's sketchbook and began to flip through it.

"Oh, my stars!" she exclaimed. "What in the world are you drawing?"

Becky snatched the sketchbook out of her cousin's hand and held it tightly to her. "None of your beeswax."

"Aunt Kitty, you should see the things Becky is drawing. Disgusting. I dare say downright porno-graphic," Fanny said, her eyes squinting and her lips pulled down at the sides.

"Rebecca, what have you done now to get your poor cousin in such a state?" Kitty asked, barely listening as she handed all the packages and shop-ping bags to Moxley to stuff into the rumble seat.

"If you must know—" Becky's mind flew with lies to tell her mother. If only she were alone with Fanny, she'd threaten to knock her block off if she spoke a word of her drawings to anyone. But when was Fanny ever known to keep a confidence? Never, as far as Becky could remember.

"Yes, I must," Kitty replied as she climbed into the front sat, Moxley shutting the door tightly behind her.

"I was drawing my interpretation of the recent string of murders," Becky admitted. It was the truth, but when she spoke it, she thought it didn't sound nearly that gruesome.

Kitty let out a long sigh. "Must you be so morbid?"

"You should see them, Aunt Kitty. Why, I can only imagine the things people would say if anyone laid eyes on such filth."

"First of all, it isn't filth," Becky said. "Second, no one looks at my sketchbooks. They are for my hobby only. You were snooping." Becky lifted her chin, hoping her mother wouldn't ask to see them. They were graphic, but Becky had no control over it. She barely recalled drawing them, since she was reliving her nightmare.

"All right, both of you!" Kitty exclaimed. "Poor

Moxley has got to have a throbbing head since we all climbed in the car! You'd swear you two were bona fide sisters the way you quarrel. I'm tired of it. I don't want to hear a peep from either one of you until we get home."

Becky rolled her eyes and held tightly to her sketchbook. Fanny folded her arms over her chest and looked away from Becky to watch the scenery slip by. The rest of the ride home was in silence, and Becky was grateful for it. It was twisting in her gut how her mother let Fanny off the hook so many times. There was never any talk about manners or being ladylike to Fanny, who was as tactful as a bull in a pasture of heifers.

Once they were home, Becky scrambled to get out of the car, grab her bags, and march upstairs, but her mother stopped her before she could make a clean getaway. She got pinched. In all her close calls sneaking out windows and back doors of speakeasies being raided by the cops, Becky was never so nervous as she was now.

"Rebecca, let me see your sketchbook," Kitty said quickly.

"Mama, these are my drawings. I don't show them to anyone," Becky protested.

"You won't believe it, Aunt Kitty. If I were you, I would..."

"You are not me, Fanny. Go on into the house," Kitty snapped.

Once her cousin and Moxley were in the house, Becky handed over her drawings like she was turning over a sack of diamonds she'd stolen from a safe. Kitty flipped through it. Becky watched her swallow hard and then look at her daughter.

"Mama, they are just sketches. The papers are running these stories every day. To ignore them would be like saying those poor people who have been killed didn't matter. The whole point of art is to..."

"Rebecca, I'm shocked. Isn't it bad enough you spend your days lurking around that cemetery doing heaven knows what? Are you drawing things you see in there too?" Kitty put her hand to her throat.

Becky straightened her back and glared at her mother. "Yes. I do draw things I see in there. The morning glories that grow around the worn-down fence. The Spanish moss that is home to birds and insects of all colors. And especially the tombstones of the people who have long been forgotten by the fine people of Savannah, just like these people will be." She pointed at her sketchbook, which her mother was still holding.

"Becky, I worry about you so much. You are so different than everyone else. You don't seem to fit in, and what is going to happen..." Kitty started but bit her lip.

"What is going to happen when?" Becky asked.

"What is going to happen when Martha and Teddy get married and decide to move away? What's going to happen when your father and I are no longer here to take care of you? You must set these strange habits and hobbies aside and learn to be a normal young lady."

"I've done everything you've ever asked, Mama. I've entertained the young men you've tried to saddle me with. I've never given in to any rumors or scandals that would bring shame to the MacKenzie name. I've been a good daughter. Maybe your question should be what you are going to do when I've decided to move away. Oh, I don't think it will be an issue. You'll have Fanny here to take my place," Becky snapped.

She'd never spoken to her mother this way before. Once all the words were out, Becky stretched out her hand for her mother to hand over her sketchbook. Kitty did so but said nothing more.

Without hesitating, Becky walked into the house only to find Fanny pretending to be browsing through a magazine within earshot of the whole conversation. Still, Becky said nothing and went upstairs. It was a shock to herself when she realized that for most of the day, she hadn't thought of Adam White once. But Herbert had crossed her mind. More than once.

CHAPTER 8

*S*everal days had passed since Fanny exposed Becky's drawings to her mother. During that time, she had only one good night's sleep, and that was because she'd forced herself to stay up late trying to mend a hem that she'd torn. The other nights were restless. She'd wake up and be unable to drift off again, tossing and turning like there was something she was missing or had forgotten to tend to before going to sleep, like a candle left burning somewhere or laundry left out on the line. Of course, there was no such task left unattended.

But the worst was the night of her awful dream. The same two characters she'd seen at Cecelia's were in it, clinging to the shadows as Becky ran like a wild woman through the tobacco plants. She didn't dare tell anyone about it. Instead, she drew the picture in her sketchbook. She tried to recall every little detail, no matter how unnerving. But there weren't many. Just the dark figures and the tobacco plants. This time, she hid her sketchbook deep in the back of her armoire. It was funny how no one really took too much of an interest in her drawings until she was drawing something they didn't like. The violation was still fresh. It made for quiet meals at the dining room table, where most of the conversation came from Fanny, who was all too happy to be in the spotlight.

Judge, who never shied away from a conversation among the ladies of the house, had been distracted himself. There was a patch of tobacco in the field that had an infestation of brown stink bugs. They were devastating to tobacco plants. Although Judge had said he was sure he got them under control before they could do any real damage, it would occupy his mind until he knew for sure.

This particular morning, Becky spoke in one-word answers and excused herself after only a couple of bites. She was sure she heard a familiar sound rolling up the driveway. Before anyone could stop her, she was out the front door waving at

Teddy, who was pulling up in his Flivver, which shined under the hot Savannah sun.

"Guess what I saw just rolling into town at the very tippy-tip of the Rockdale Estate?" he said as he hopped out of the car, tipping his straw hat down over his eyebrows.

"Let me guess. Those amazing young men and their flying machine?" Becky said as she stepped on the running board.

"Not quite. But wouldn't that be something?" Teddy leaned on the hood. "A carnival."

"Really?" Becky's eyes bugged. "Let's go watch them set up. That's always been more fascinating than the carnival itself."

"You were reading my mind, doll. Uh, do you need to ask your cousin Fanny to come along? You know, just to pass the peace pipe?" Teddy asked behind the back of his hand. Becky glared at him, her right eyebrow arching high up on her forehead. "Yikes. That look could peel paint. Sorry I asked. Get in. We'll make a quick getaway."

Becky did just that, and before she knew it, they were at the edge of Teddy's family estate, where off in the distance a row of striped booths and small tents were popping up like toadstools.

"Remember when we used to walk all this way when we were kids?" Becky reminisced.

"What are you talking about? You still are a kid," Teddy teased.

"My mother makes me feel like I am. And standing next to Fanny... that makes me look like one," Becky huffed.

"Uh-oh. Trouble in paradise. Come on. Spill the beans. Tell Uncle Teddy your problems."

Becky shook her head. "It's such a nice day. I don't want to ruin it."

"Nonsense." Teddy put the car in park and cut the engine. Before Becky could protest, he pulled a blanket from the back seat and a flask from his pocket. He walked to the front of the car and offered her his elbow.

"How can I say no to you?" she said with a chuckle.

"You can't. Come on. Let's get closer to the action," Teddy insisted. As they walked, Becky did reminisce about the times when they were kids and would spend all day exploring their properties, which both seemed to go on forever. She was positive there wasn't an inch of ground they hadn't covered together at one time or another.

When they were close enough to the carnival site

to hear people talking, they stopped, spread out their blanket on the grass, and took a seat. It didn't take long for Becky to ask for the flask. She tipped her head back and took a small sip. The gin tasted pleasantly bitter under the hot sun.

"So, what's bothering you?" Teddy asked before taking a sip himself.

Becky took a deep breath and told Teddy the story. The whole story. Visiting Cecelia. The drawing she wasn't even aware she was doing. Then, Fanny's discovery of the scribbles of the crime scene she'd dreamt about. Teddy listened intently without interrupting until Becky was finished. She was out of breath by the time she got everything out.

"Am I crazy, Teddy? Did I overreact?"

Teddy took another swig from his flask then passed it to her. "No, doll. In fact, I think that Fanny ought to get a lesson in what happens to snitches." He sniffed, swiped the side of his nose with his thumb, and gave Becky a wink.

"I swear, sometimes I wish she'd take a long walk off a short pier," Becky added.

"But I'd like to know more about this dream you had. What's that all about, Beck? I know you have some specialties with the folks still hanging around the Old Brick Cemetery. Plus, a couple of other tricks up your sleeve. But this sounds like a new one."

"I don't know. You remember that guy off skid row who came up to me at Willie's? It seems like ever since that happened, I've had a string of bad luck following me. Not nearly as bad as the poor bums who have been murdered. But this is no cakewalk, Teddy. In fact, I had another one last night." Becky confessed.

"Another what?"

"Nightmare."

"What happened?"

Becky went on to describe two men fighting not far from a twisted tree adorned with Spanish moss like most of the trees in Savannah. That same voice hissed in the background.

"But this time, they didn't leave the poor dope for the train to finish off. When the man was out cold, they did something I couldn't make out. They hovered over him like maybe they were trying to get him breathing again or giving him a crack or two to see if he'd come around. But after that, I woke up." Becky looked out at the buzzing carnies, who had already erected three more attractions since she and Teddy had sat down. The smell of burning wood wafted over from a thin line of black smoke curling its way around itself like a snake into the sky. The sound of hammers hitting nails and rails could be heard in a steady rhythm while men shouted orders and retorts to one another. Occasionally, a snippet of music or a burst of laughter came from the camp that was getting bigger and bigger as the sun crept across the sky.

"Did you see anything in the papers about the coppers finding another body?" Teddy asked.

"My mother's been hiding the morning paper from me. She thinks it's what's giving me the heebie-jeebies." Becky smirked.

"Well, in a case like this, no news is good news. Maybe your mother is right. Maybe if you avoid the paper and the news about these killings, you won't dream about them. It wouldn't be the worst thing, Beck."

"But what about my drawings? Cecelia walked me through it. She said it's another gift. Let me tell you, I'm getting tired of the Santa Claus routine. I'd welcome a bag of coal instead of all this," Becky said, making Teddy laugh.

"I'm not saying you didn't draw them from some-where deep in that noggin of yours. I'm just saying that the murders have been on everyone's mind lately. Madame Cecelia could probably pull out a couple of doodles from me and the man on the moon too." Teddy squinted at the workers who were standing around a pole having a smoke not far from where they were sitting.

"I don't think I'd be so jittery if it weren't for Fanny. She dropped the dime on me like I was Henry Moity," Becky snapped. She stretched her legs out in front of her and crossed them at the ankles while leaning back, her arms behind her, propping her up.

"You're letting her get the best of you. Put her on ice. Keep your distance for a while. She'll start to blend into the woodwork, and you won't even know she's around," Teddy said before taking a sip from his flask and passing it to Becky.

"Not know Fanny is around? Are you off your rocker? How can you miss her?" Becky said, looking down at the flask.

"You might find this hard to believe, but we men do like the skirts with a little action between the ears. And you got that in spades, baby," Teddy added with a wink.

"You've always been a darb, Teddy. Just a swell guy. I don't know where I'd be if it weren't for you," Becky said then took a sip.

"I know where you'd be. In the Old Brick Cemetery, dry as a bone because none of the residents have a flask they can share," Teddy teased.

They chatted for a little while longer about the carnival and the upcoming annual festivities at the Potts' residence.

"You are going, right?" Becky asked as they stood up from their blanket and dusted off the dry grass from their clothes. Becky had the feeling they were being watched. When she looked up at the carnival that was now a humming mini-town of heavy cloth tents, brightly colored booths, and stiff-standing rides that would come to life when the sun went down, she couldn't help but notice a couple of Brunos standing there watching them.

"Wouldn't miss it."

"Say, what do you think those hammerheads are looking at?" Becky asked, jerking her head toward a handful of carnies looking in their direction.

"Are you kidding? They'll stop the presses to see a pretty girl like you walk by any day. What are they looking at? *You*, my dear," Teddy replied.

Becky chuckled and waved. All the men smiled and waved back before turning and getting back to work. The biggest one in the middle looked over his shoulder at her once more before he disappeared behind a tent.

"You know what? I think I'm going to walk home," Becky said. "It's cooler today, and I'd like to remember those times when we were kids a little longer. Our path through the trees and along that little crick is still there, I'm sure."

"I hate the idea of leaving you out here alone," Teddy said as they walked to the car. He dumped the blanket in the back seat and tucked his now-empty flask in his pocket.

"Drive me to the edge of the trees. It's only a hop, skip, and jump to the MacKenzie property line. I'll probably find Daddy out there making sure the doodlebugs or boll weevils aren't eating his crops."

"Boll weevils eat cotton plants. Let's not sound like an ignoramus," Teddy teased, rolling his eyes. Becky gave him a jab in the gut before she hopped in the passenger seat.

"You don't want to drive?" Teddy asked before getting behind the wheel.

"No one likes a wise guy, Theodore," Becky replied. Within seconds they were off the way they'd come, jostling around in the Flivver, the warm wind in their faces. Once at the edge of the trees, Teddy stopped the car.

"All right, dollface. Here's your stop. Don't take any wooden nickels."

"I'll try and remember that. Drinks and dancing tomorrow?" she asked before slamming the car door shut.

"Does a bear shi—"

"That'll do, Theodore! See you tomorrow." Becky laughed as she scurried toward the well-worn path that she and Teddy had traveled a million times when they were kids. Before swinging at speakeasies became the rage. The sputter of the Flivver kicked in as Teddy shifted gears, and the tires kicked up the dirt before he drove off. Becky felt better after seeing him alone like when they were young. Teddy was her first friend, and Martha was her best. The three of them had so many good times together that Becky felt blessed. Of course, so many of those times also included Adam.

As she walked, Becky recalled her last time with Adam. He was as handsome as ever, but the words he spoke still stung the very core of her heart. No matter how much she tried to pretend she was getting over him, she wasn't. Herbert was a wonderful distraction and so different from anyone she'd ever gone out with. But deep down, she was worried that was all he was. A distraction. A rebound. That made her feel a little guilty, since she was sure she was going to see him again at some time. Plus, she was sure she'd have a great time with him. Heck, according to Fanny, he was quite the dancer. That was something Becky wanted to see for herself.

"Maybe tomorrow," she muttered as she walked the path.

Her shoes were not made for the rough terrain, and in short order, her toes started to feel pinched. There was no way she'd be able to dance tomorrow if she continued walking this way. A fallen log was just up ahead. Becky took a seat and within seconds removed her shoes and stockings, which had already had a run in them. The dirt path was cool beneath her feet, and the grass tickled at her ankles. Birds chirped overhead, and the sound of the brook could be heard bubbling just up ahead. Becky loved to search for brightly colored rocks and stones made smooth by the water. Just because she was an adult didn't change that. Once at the water's edge, she looked around before hiking up her skirt and stepping into the cold water. The stones were smooth beneath her feet and massaged her toes that had been aching just a few seconds ago.

After a couple steps, Becky found a beautifully smooth stone that was no bigger than a penny, orange in color. She plucked it out of the dirt and sand and studied it up close. Looking down, she took a few more steps before something green caught her eye. It didn't sparkle. It was just a color that looked out of place. Everything around was so muted that Becky hardly realized she was looking at the fingernail of a hand that was submerged in water.

Her breath caught in her throat without her even realizing it. Without blinking, she followed up the hand to an arm in a tattered and faded dress shirt and jacket. The rest of the man was covered by the leaves of the plants that grew in lush patches along the edge of the water.

"Mister?" Becky called. "Are you all right? This is no place to doze off."

There was no response. Somewhere deep in the back of Becky's mind, she knew she wasn't going to get a reply.

Maybe he's on a bender. Or maybe the heat of the last few hot days overtook him, she thought, knowing full well that resting from the heat or recuperating from a night out didn't turn the fingernails purple. She looked at the hand again. It didn't stir in the slightest as the water rippled over it.

Before stepping closer, Becky looked around and found a long stick. Trying not to disrupt the water, just in case the man was still alive, she leaned and stretched far enough to snatch up the stick from the ground on the other side of the bank. She regained her footing, held the stick in both hands, and carefully nudged one of the fingers. Still nothing happened.

"Mister? Do you need some help?"

No, Rebecca, he needs a mortician. This is a stiff, as stiff as they get. Scram before the jakes that did this give you a dry-gulch too.

But Becky couldn't. She didn't think the guy suffered a blow to the head so someone could take his money. His clothes were worn out. His hand looked big and rough. This was a ragamuffin. Just like the man who had found her at Willie's and the boxing match.

With trembling hands, Becky used the stick to push aside the grass and growth that was hiding the rest of his body.

What do you need to see for? You know he's dead. You've seen a person who croaked before. You've seen one stiff, you've seen them all, her mind was shouting, but still she inched forward.

As she separated the grass, Becky could make out that the man's shirt had been torn open. On his chest were several suction marks, like he'd had a couple of leeches sucking on him. That was bad enough. When she looked to his face, she didn't see it. Oh, it was there. The head was there with the eyes open and staring blankly in her direction. But it had been almost completely removed from the rest of the body.

CHAPTER 9

*B*ecky ran all the way home. Somewhere along the way, she dropped her shoes. Perhaps they were by the body. Maybe they fell in the water. She couldn't remember. All she could see were that poor man's eyes staring ahead like he was expecting someone to come and help. At the thought of such loneliness, Becky's heart ached. But there would be time to mourn the poor man, and that time wasn't now. *Now* the only thing on her mind was getting away from that scene. Becky was sure that had she been timed, she would have broken some kind of record covering the distance from the brook to her property faster than a bolt of lightning could strike the ground. Fortunately, her father was at the edge of the tobacco field, and he was checking the plants for bugs when she burst through the rows of tobacco toward him. He caught her in his big strong arms.

"My gosh, Becky! What's eating you? Where are your shoes?" her father asked.

Becky gulped at the air and pointed behind her, but the words couldn't get past her panting. The foreman brought her a ladle of water that she gulped down. Judge practically had to hold her up as she tried to catch her breath after she'd wiped the water that had trickled over her mouth and chin. Finally, she spilled the beans.

"Daddy, there's a man," she started.

Immediately Judge's face became grim. His daughter came running through the tobacco plants. Her shoes were missing, and her hair was messed. It was only natural he would assume that there was a masher on his property. Becky could tell immediately this was what her father thought. She didn't want to blurt it out in front of his hired hands. Some of them were dreadfully superstitious. But she had no choice. If she didn't, Judge and his men would open fire on anyone who might just be drifting through.

"Get my rifle, Mr. Charles," Judge said to the foreman. Becky gulped and patted her father's chest.

"Daddy, this man is… dead. Dead as a doornail. He's lying just off the edge of the creek about a quarter mile." She pointed in the direction she'd come from.

"Mr. Charles, you come with me. Becky, I want you to go back to the house. You know all the boys here. Fellas, make sure she gets to Miss Kitty," Judge ordered and received a nod of agreement from each man.

Becky did know them all. She made it a point to know her father's employees. Most of them were more interesting than half the people who paid a casual visit to the MacKenzie plantation.

"What did you see, Miss Becky?"

"Did you know the man?"

"That's an awful fright for a woman."

The men talked more than Becky did. She told them just that she'd found a body and that the man looked like a hobo. She didn't give any of the gruesome details. But she didn't have to. The men had heard throughout town that there had been a string of vagabonds being killed. One of the men said it was a maniac who picked on the down-and-out.

"Those people got enough troubles. Some suffer from the drink. Others got their marbles shook from the Great War," one man Becky knew as Jimmy said.

"Some are just lazy. You don't know. This feller could have stolen pies from Miss Lucy's windowsill just this month," the second man chimed in. He wore a red kerchief around his neck that he'd pull up to wipe the sweat from his lip.

"It's a sign. Bad mojo," the last man said. Becky felt a shiver run across her shoulders as she watched him pull a crucifix from around his neck and hold it tightly for a few seconds. "Something has been prowling these parts. I don't reckon it's going to stop any time soon neither."

"What do you think it is?" Becky asked.

"Don't know. Don't want to know," the man replied.

After that, a lively discussion of what happened erupted. Becky was happy to just listen. She didn't dare tell them of her dreams. Her father wouldn't have a soul left to help him tend the crops. But her last nightmare hit too close to home. It wasn't any of her kin that was there lying on the ground torn apart. But it was a poor man down on his luck. Maybe he did suffer from drink, as Jimmy had said. Had he come to her father for a job, Judge would have given it to him. Plus, he'd have had a good talking-to and a safe place to stay while he got on his feet.

That was the thing about Judge MacKenzie. He knew not to assume what a man was made of just by the way he looked. If he worked hard, if he spoke kindly, if he believed in the Almighty, then he was a man Judge would be proud to have on his payroll. Judge had raised his daughter to think the same way. At least, he tried to. Guilt over the way she acted toward the hobo who had come up to her in Willie's and on her date with Herbert settled in her chest. What if she'd listened to him? Maybe she could have helped. Maybe she could have gotten him off the sauce and into a job on the plantation. Maybe he'd still be alive.

"Maybe this man just slipped and hit his head. Killed himself," the man with the kerchief said. Becky didn't dare open her mouth and tell him it must have been a very sharp rock to separate his noggin from his shoulders.

"Nope. This is bad mojo," the man with the crucifix said.

"All right, boys. No need to be scaring Miss Becky. She's had enough of a fright today. Ain't that right, Miss Becky. Listen to us fools talking about such grim things," Jimmy said. "Didn't I see you with a new fella the other day?"

Becky chuckled. Leave it to her father's hired

hands to know everything going on at the MacKenzie plantation.

"Yes," she replied while shaking her head.

"He's a real alderman. Can't say it looks like he ever skipped a meal," Jimmy joked while patting his gut.

"It's true. He's a little heavy. But he's swell. A good egg." Becky smiled.

"As long as he treats you right, Miss Becky, we won't have a problem. Look." Jimmy pointed at the clearing of the tobacco plants where Kitty was outside on the porch with Lucretia in the yard hanging laundry. They were chatting casually as the quartet walked up.

"Thanks for the escort, boys. I can make it from here," Becky said.

"You take care now, Miss Becky!" The men all waved before turning and heading back toward the edge of the field where Judge and Mr. Charles had headed off.

Becky waved back and waited until they were out of sight. She turned and saw her mother looking at her with more worry on her face. Even though Becky had long ago stopped running to her mother when there was a problem, confident she'd be able to solve things on her own, there were times she felt like a little girl and needed the woman desperately. Now was one of those times. With tears in her eyes, she hurried to Kitty.

"My dear, what's the matter? Where are your shoes?" Kitty asked.

"Mama, there's been an accident," Becky started.

As she did with the hired hands, she left out the gory details. But she told her mother of the poor man next to the creek. Kitty just listened, and once all the facts were out, she took Becky by the hand, sat down on the porch swing, and held her as she cried. Becky cried for the poor man, for the other men who were the prey of such a monster. She also cried for herself and the curse she was under that had her see these things before they happened. Something she could tell no one.

CHAPTER 10

*a*bout an hour later, Becky heard a car rolling up the driveway. Her first thought was hopeful it was Herbert. She was rather surprised at herself for allowing him to pop into her mind after such a day. Kitty had suggested she go upstairs and lie down. Becky did as she was told, even though the last thing on her mind was getting in a catnap. Instead, she looked at her sketchbook and saw so many things that matched this incident that she began to tremble. But the sound of rolling tires meant someone was here to change the feeling in the air. Becky would have welcomed any of the horse-toothed, cock-eyed beaus her mother had set her up with over the past several months over nothing.

But when she peeked out her window, she saw

the police car. Her father must have made it home and called them. Just then there was a rap on the door.

"Come in," Becky replied.

Kitty peeked her head in. "Darling, the police are here. They'd like to talk to you about this afternoon. If you don't feel like visitors, I can have them come back another time."

"No, Mama. I'd like to get this over with," Becky replied. "I'm sorry I lost my shoes. And I ruined another pair of stockings."

Kitty couldn't help but chuckle. "Did I ever tell you the time I went out with your father before we were married and came home with only one shoe on?"

Becky's eyes bugged out of her head. "Mama!"

Kitty shook her head. "You go on now and talk with the officer. I'll tell you that tale later."

"You're darn right you will," Becky chirped as she slipped past her mama and headed downstairs. Of course, Fanny was there already, flipping her hair and going on about how the police uniforms in Paris were so much different from the ones here in Savannah. She blathered on like the crimes in France were somehow classier than the crimes committed here. Becky wondered if Fanny could possibly be more annoying. The sad truth was she'd find out, and the answer would be yes.

"Why, Becky, I haven't seen you in some time," the officer said with a smile. Becky had seen him on more than one occasion, letting her slip out of a raid or two and sometimes even sharing a dance at a speakeasy when he was off duty. A pleasant gent by the name of Shoemacher.

"Why Officer Daniel Shoemacher, had I known you'd be showing up at my door, I'd have spotted some ornery character on the property weeks ago," Becky said as she reached out to shake his hand.

"You two know each other?" Kitty asked as she entered the room. Judge stood against the wall, his pipe glowing and a steady stream of smoke curling up around his head. He looked worried.

"We've bumped into each other a time or two. Isn't that right, Officer?" Becky replied.

"Savannah can be a small town at times. Unfortunately, it's big enough to have its rough spots. Becky, can you tell me what happened?" Officer Shoemacher said as he pulled a small notebook and a stump of pencil from his pocket.

"Maybe we should walk a little, Officer. Is that all right, Daddy?"

Judge nodded solemnly. He looked at Kitty, who was wringing her hands with worry.

Becky nodded and before going out touched her mother's arm. She hated to see her fret. Officer Shoemacher held the screen door as Becky stepped out on the porch. They walked slowly to the edge of the tobacco field.

Becky took her time explaining how she and Teddy had gone to watch the carnies setting up the festival in the field off the ends of the property. Without hesitation, she told how she'd been walking that path alone and with Teddy for so many years, she couldn't recall. There had never been any kind of incident. As far as she knew, no one but them knew about the path or was even interested in it.

"It's not like it was a shortcut to some juke joint or moonshine distillery," Becky said with a wink. Having a drink next to a copper was not unheard of, and Becky knew how to keep a secret. She always thought of it as an ace in her pocket if she ever got in a serious jam. "I don't know what business the man had roaming back there. But whatever he was doing back there... Officer Shoemacher. What were those marks on his chest? The other victims had them, too, didn't they?"

"We kept that detail out of the papers so we'd

know what we were dealing with. I don't need to tell you to keep it under your hat," the officer whispered.

"What are they?"

Officer Shoemacher swallowed hard, looked out across the field at the stalks of tobacco, then put his notebook and pencil back in his pocket. "We don't know. All we do know is that the men barely put up any kind of fight. It's like they were weak as kittens. No attempt to defend themselves. No bruises on the knuckles or blood under the fingers from scratching. Nothing. It's like all they could do was lie down and... let this happen."

"Like they were on a bender?"

"No. Like they were drained. Drained of all their energy or will to even live. It's a lot of applesauce, Becky." The officer shook his head. "Do me a favor, would you?"

"Ab-so-tively, Officer," Becky replied and looked up at the uniformed copper.

"Don't go out alone. Stick with the gang, and if you have to go stag, call a cab. Would you do that for me?" Officer Shoemacher asked.

"That's my usual routine, Shoemacher. I'm no greenhorn," Becky replied.

"Same goes for your cousin." He jerked his thumb toward the house, where Fanny was not-sodiscreetly sitting on the porch, fanning herself with a paper fan, swinging lazily in the porch swing. She was pretending not to listen, but if she leaned any farther to the side, she'd be kissing the wooden floor.

"Don't worry about her. She's never at a loss for some Bruno to take her home," Becky replied without regard to sounding petty.

"Yeah, but if she's not a dumb Dora, I don't know what is. Stick together," Officer Shoemacher replied.

"You have no idea what you're asking." Becky chuckled.

"Will you promise?"

"Of course. She might need a pop in the chops sometimes, but I don't want this to happen to her. I don't want it to happen to anyone," Becky added. After a few more minutes of chewing the fat, Becky shook Officer Shoemacher's hand before he turned toward his car. Judge hurried down the porch steps to talk to him in private as Becky went back up to the house.

"You certainly had a quiet conversation. Makes me think you two were talking about more than what you found in the woods," Fanny said as Becky took a seat on the porch.

"Do you ever mind your own beeswax? There has been a rash of killings, and all you're worried about is who I'm talking to. You sure are some piece of work, Fanny. A real Rembrandt."

"It's not like you haven't given your poor mother enough to worry about with those obscene drawings in your sketchbook, but..."

Luckily, the sound of another car approaching down the long dirt road to the MacKenzie house distracted them both. Becky recognized it right away and had to admit she was happy to see it. Herbert's Flivver. The argument would have to wait. Becky knew it wasn't like there wasn't going to be another one.

She stood up and waved as he approached. Judge was still chatting with Officer Shoemacher when Herbert cut the engine and approached. He looked at Becky, concerned, and again surprised her with how agilely he moved, as if that alderman he carried around his middle was of no consequence.

Before Becky could say anything, Fanny was up and leaning forward over the railing like she was on a boat suffering seasickness.

"No one told me you were paying a visit," Fanny chirped.

"Hello, Fanny. I do hope the police are here on a friendly visit. Becky, is everything copacetic?" he asked, looking past Fanny like she wasn't even there.

Becky smirked and wanted to hug the big galoot for it. But she contained herself and greeted him at the steps instead.

"It's been an exciting day. How about I get you a glass of lemonade and we chew the fat all about it," Becky replied.

"That sounds ducky. Is that your father?" Herbert asked.

"Sure is," Becky replied proudly.

"He's a big man," Herbert replied.

"In more ways than one. You have a seat. I'll tell Mama you're here," Becky said and hurried into the house. She heard Fanny start babbling as soon as she left the porch. Something about the heat and the police being called and her utter devastation that a body was found on their property. Becky didn't know what ruffled her feathers more. That Fanny was singing like a canary about the poor dead hobo or that she called it *their property*. She had no claim to the MacKenzie plantation and shouldn't be referring to it as such.

"Let her blow, Rebecca. She's nothing but a bag of wind. Herbert is smart enough to sniff that out," she said to herself before informing her mother of his arrival and asking for some lemonade.

"Herbert, what a pleasant surprise." With a wide

smile and a hearty handshake, Kitty welcomed him and said she'd bring the lemonade out in a few minutes.

"So, what's all the hubbub, bub?" Herbert asked as he eased himself into the rocking chair next to the swing on the porch. "You found a dead person on your property?"

Becky told Herbert how she came to discover the poor sap. Fanny sat in the swing, still fanning herself, looking bored and uninterested in the whole matter, and instead focused on Judge, who was still talking with Officer Shoemacher.

"I don't like this," Herbert said.

"Me either. I've got a hinky feeling about the whole situation," Becky replied.

"I don't mean about that. I mean about you spending time with another cat. I know you mentioned Teddy before. His squeeze is Martha, right?" Herbert said with a sly smirk. "Maybe he should be chinning with her."

Becky stared at Herbert before starting to laugh. "You've got to be daft! Teddy's kin! Don't be a wise-cracker!"

"Teddy does spend a lot of time here. You have to admit it," Fanny interrupted.

"Fanny? Can you come and help Lucretia in the

kitchen, please?" Kitty said as she opened the porch door with her hip, carrying a tray with two glasses and a pitcher of lemonade.

"Oh, but I'm entertaining our guest with…"

"Becky can handle things. Thank you, dear," Kitty ordered sweetly. Fanny pinched her lips together and forced a smile.

"I do hope you won't leave without saying good-bye," Fanny said, stooping down to give Herbert as much of a view of her bosom as she could with Kitty ready to throw ice on her at any moment.

"Nice to see you, Fanny," Herbert replied like he was a politician who ran into the person running against him in an upcoming election. As soon as he was alone with Becky on the porch, each of them with a lemonade in their hands, Herbert became serious.

"Someday my cousin will leave this house, and I have the feeling that no matter how hard I try… I won't be able to stop smiling," Becky whispered before giggling. But Herbert barely grinned. She stared at him for a second before asking what the matter was.

"Oh, I hate to admit it, but I've got a jealous bone."

"You do? Over Teddy?"

Herbert shrugged. "I can't help it, Becky. I think you're the cat's pajamas."

Becky grinned and looked over the edge of the porch. She'd never been so flattered. There was just something about Herbert's expression, the way he said the words, that made her almost forget what she'd seen earlier. Almost. Becky hated to admit that if the dead man had just been decapitated, he would have been easier to forget. It was those strange suction marks that stuck in her mind and truly scared her.

CHAPTER 11

The morning Becky woke up to dark circles under her eyes was the day she decided enough was enough. There was no way she could ignore the nightmares she was having anymore. They weren't just nightmares. Somewhere, something was trying to break through to her, and if she didn't get some kind of answers, she was sure whatever it was was going to kill her too.

"I always thought 'dead tired' was just an expression," she said to her reflection in the mirror as she slowly got dressed. The reception she got at the breakfast table was not a surprise.

"Becky, are you all right?" Judge asked, peeking over the top of his paper.

"My goodness, dear. You look like something the cat dragged in," Kitty said.

"I don't know what's wrong with me. I just haven't been sleeping right," Becky replied casually.

There was no way she was going to tell them that for the past three nights, she'd dreamt of a bag lady being chased down an alley only to meet her doom.

"Well, I've been sleeping just fine," Fanny said before taking a bite of grits. "In fact, I don't think I've ever slept better. Nothing ages a person quicker than not getting the proper sleep. All the ladies in Paris insisted that ten hours of rest was what a lady should have."

"Maybe you should take that information and shove—" Becky started.

"Rebecca," Judge interrupted. "That Herbert fellow seems nice. I was mighty impressed with him the other day. A good firm handshake. Looks a fellow right in the eye. Your mama's told me he's been quite the gentleman with you."

"Yes," Becky replied. She was annoyed and glared at Fanny. Of course, her lack of sleep didn't help her temper.

"He might be just the fellow to escort you to the Potts' annual picnic. He's very personable. And there will be lots of food there. I'm sure he'll be made to feel right at home," Judge added while patting his belly.

"Yes, he's a bit on the portly side," Becky admitted.

"I'm not saying that's a bad thing. On the contrary, a man with a little meat on his bones is obviously eating well. A father wants his daughter to be with a man who will provide. I hear he took you to the Silver Club. Didn't hide the menu from you, did he?"

"No, Daddy." Becky let out a sigh.

"Then he wants you to eat well too. Good on him." Judge chuckled.

"I eat just fine." Becky rolled her eyes as she poured herself coffee from the silver pot on the table.

"He took you to the Silver Club?" Fanny cleared her throat.

"Yes" was all Becky replied. She knew that Fanny had aspirations to go to the Silver Club with some Bruno with more brawn than brains and a wallet full of cabbage. "Just think, it could have been you if you hadn't been so nasty to Herbert when you first met him."

"What?" Kitty gasped. "Fanny, is that true? Did he make advances on you?"

"Calm down, Kitty," Judge said, patting both Becky's and Fanny's hands. "We've got the two most beautiful girls in Savannah under the same roof. It won't be the last time a gent takes one for a spin and then another. Besides, Becky, how many of the fellows in Savannah have you had a dance with?"

"Just about all of them, Daddy," Becky replied then took a bite of the toast she'd just buttered.

Normally, she'd be fussing and snapping with her father and Fanny that there was nothing to Herbert's flirting and that he'd told her all about it. But her mind was so sluggish the only thing to come out of her mouth after that was a garbled *"Were handled prscrib filly."* She had no idea what it meant and was sure she'd dozed off at the table for a second.

As the conversation among her father, Kitty, and Cousin Fanny continued, Becky decided she needed a trip downtown. Cecelia had to have something that would help her sleep or at least chase away the nightmares. The fact that every time she had one, another transient was found dead was too much for her to face. It was just coincidence.

You don't believe in coincidences, Rebecca. Even the voice in her head was crabby.

The problem would be getting downtown with no one tagging along. The last thing she wanted was for Fanny to hear this conversation and report back to Mama that Becky needed to be sized up for a straitjacket.

But as luck would have it, Lucretia came to the rescue. "Miss Kitty. It looks like we are plumb out of brown sugar, and I am in the middle of making an apple pie. Do you think..."

"I can run to the Rockdales' and borrow a cup or two," Becky offered.

"You were reading my mind." Lucretia smiled.

"I'll go right now," Becky said, taking one last gulp of coffee and pushing herself away from the table before Kitty or Judge could suggest she take her cousin. The walk in the fresh air and sunshine did her some good as she cut through the grass to the Rockdale property. The heat had subsided for the time being, and a blanket of soft, light clouds covered the sun as a cool breeze rustled the tall weeds.

Suddenly, Becky had the strangest feeling that she wasn't alone. Looking over her shoulder, she half expected to see Fanny wobbling up behind her in her heels, trying not to get even the thinnest blade of grass on her skirt. But there was no one. Looking around, she could see the rows of tobacco and the tree line that concealed the small brook where the poor hobo had been found. Finally, the Rockdale home was in view. It was a beautiful place, even bigger than the MacKenzie estate, but it was as comforting a sight as her own home. She hurried up the path and to the front door, where she knocked loudly.

"What a pleasant surprise," Mrs. Rockdale squealed. "Rebecca MacKenzie, I feel I haven't seen you in ages. And look how pretty you look today."

"Thank you, ma'am." Becky smiled and hugged Mrs. Rockdale. She asked for the sugar and was invited to sit for a spell and enjoy a glass of lemonade.

"I'd love to, but Lucretia is in the middle of making a pie. She'll have kittens if I make her ruin her recipe lollygagging. Can I take a rain check?" Becky asked.

"Of course. But I'll be looking forward to a nice long visit," Mrs. Rockdale replied.

"I know that voice," Teddy said from down the hall. He appeared in a smart striped jacket and two-toned spats.

"Don't you look as sweet as a cup of cream. Going to see Martha?" Becky asked.

"That's right. I can't let a carnival go by without trying to win my best girl a prize." Teddy winked before grabbing his straw hat from the rack by the door. After discovering Becky's reason for popping by, she pulled Teddy aside and asked him for a favor.

"Of course, diddums. I'll take you to see the gypsies. We'll pick up Martha on the way and…"

"No. I've got to go back with the sugar for Lucretia. Wait for me when the sun starts to set. I'll meet you at the end of the driveway," Becky replied.

"Sure. But why all the cloak-and-dagger?"

"I don't want anyone tagging along." Becky winked and put her finger to the side of her nose.

"Ah, yes. You don't need a Fanny *butting* in," Teddy said, winking back and chuckling at his own joke. "Done and done. See you at sundown."

As tired as she was, Becky couldn't even take a nap. She was afraid to drift off and be back in that alley with that poor woman. The worst part was that she'd been down that alley. She was sure of it. There were very few parts of Savannah that Becky didn't know. Speakeasies popped up all the time in the backs of stores, restaurants, and even a bank. Sometimes just getting into the place was a bigger challenge than getting a drink.

She was sure she'd been in the place, and if she had been, that meant it could have just as easily been her who got bumped off. So she stayed awake in her room and sat by the window daydreaming until the sun started to set. With her sketchbook in her lap, she drew little doodles of the flowers growing around the trellis of her window. She sketched the dress that was draped over her chair from yesterday. Then, before she could stop it, her head lolled to the side and sleep overcame her.

When she snapped to, her hand had flown across the pages of her sketchbook. These drawings were more detailed. Not only was Becky sure she'd been in the alley where the incident took place, but she was sure she'd seen the bag lady before. The old biddy went by the name Crazy Mary. She had a mouth like a sailor and had more than once told Becky and the gang exactly what she thought of them while pulling along a sack with all her worldly possessions in it.

Becky slapped her book shut, made her bed to look like she was in it with the pillows tucked under the blankets, and quickly shimmied down the trellis. With her sketchbook tucked tightly under her arm, she ran down the dirt road toward the spot she told Teddy to meet her at. Just as she got there, the bright beams of his Flivver came jostling down the road.

It didn't take long for her to hop in, kiss Martha hello, and thank Teddy for his help.

"Becky, Teddy says you've got a bee in your bonnet," Martha said, taking Becky's hand.

"It's more like a whole beehive," Becky admitted. "As if these nightmares aren't enough. But Fanny is getting worse and harder to deal with. And then there's Herbert. Do you know he suffered from the green-eyed monster over Teddy?"

"*My* Teddy?" Martha gasped.

Becky nodded. "I like Herbert. A lot. He's a barrel of monkeys to be around. But there is just something about him that isn't clicking. I don't know what it is. I just can't seem to think straight anymore. Like I'm supposed to be walking a straight line, but I'm going in circles."

"Cecelia will know what to do," Martha replied. "Can't you make this jalopy go any faster?"

"Your wish is my command," Teddy said before shifting the gears and hitting the gas. In no time, they were outside the apothecary on Bryn Mawr Avenue. But the scene was not what Becky had expected. It was like there was a giveaway of hair tonic, nylon stockings, and gin. The joint was jumping.

"Beck, are you sure you want to go in there? It looks like something the coppers are gonna bust any minute," Martha said.

"I'm with Martha, Beck. Maybe we should stop somewhere for a drink first. Let the crowd die down," Teddy suggested.

"No. I'm at the end of my rope. I can't wait any longer. If you guys want to wait here, I understand. I'll be quick." Before anyone could say another word, Becky was out of the car and setting off the jingling bells over the storefront entrance. Inside, Ophelia looked up from the counter, where she was handing what looked like a bag of tea over to an older man.

"Hi, Ophelia," Becky said more like she was asking a question rather than giving a greeting. "How's tricks?"

"Business is okay," Ophelia said. "My daughter is upstairs."

Becky looked around the store, counting over ten people inside and more setting off the bell over the door. She wrinkled her nose at Ophelia, who arched an eyebrow as if daring Becky to question her remark. If this was business doing only *okay*, people would be near rioting if it were ever to do really well. Without asking a question, Becky slipped behind the counter and hurried up the stairs to the apartment, where she found the door already open.

"Cecelia?" Becky called.

"Hello. This is a pleasant surprise," Cecelia said as

she came from the back room. Becky gasped when she saw her.

"Wow. You look like you just stepped out of a movie with Valentino," Becky chirped.

Her friend, who always wore bright colors and flowing scarves, was dressed in an exceptionally daring orange blouse with a flowing skirt that made it look like she was floating when she walked. Her thick black hair was pinned up instead of cascading down her shoulders, and her red lips were only upstaged by the intensity of her piecing dark eyes.

"Thank you. I've got a séance later this evening. A rather wealthy customer who is paying for all the bells and whistles," Cecelia replied with a wink.

"A séance? How exciting," Becky replied.

"This ought to be an interesting one. They are looking for buried inheritance," Cecelia replied as she picked up an atomizer and gave herself a couple of puffs of perfume. "It usually leads to arguments and accusations more than a map to some squirrelled-away treasure."

"I wish I could come with. That sounds like a hoot," Becky replied before casually looking down at the side table next to the sofa and tenderly touching the doily that covered it.

"You're still having nightmares, aren't you,"

Cecelia said. "I can tell by the bags under your eyes. Sleep isn't on your agenda, is it?"

Becky looked up at Cecelia and nodded. "But they are getting worse. A man was found on our property. And I keep seeing this old woman."

Becky spilled the beans to Cecelia as quickly as the words would come to her.

"I know that woman you are talking about. Crazy Mary. She's carried a lot of demons with her. I'm wondering if death wouldn't be more of a blessing for the poor creature," Cecelia muttered.

"How can you say that? If you saw what I saw, you'd see the terror in her eyes. You'd hear the horror in her voice. She isn't crazy when this happens. It's like for the last few minutes of her life she's lucid and aware and knows she's all alone. Cecelia, it's driving me crazy!" Becky didn't expect to raise her voice to her friend, but to say letting someone die—no, get *murdered*—was better than letting them live was out of the question.

"Sometimes, with these gifts we have, there are times we need to walk away. Becky, I haven't been a very good mentor when it comes to this. I've tried to help you not to be afraid and to be comfortable with your second sight and ability to communicate with the dead. But I never explained what to do when the dead become more demanding than the living."

"I can't start dealing with that now. Crazy Mary gets the big sleep soon. Maybe tonight. And I know I've seen the alley it happens in. I've got to try and stop it. But I need your help. I need you to help me see it clearer so I can get there before this monster gets a hold of her. Maybe I'll even see who it is and be able to give the police a description," Becky pleaded.

"Or maybe you'll be fit for a Chicago raincoat yourself. Did you ever think of that?" Cecelia snapped. "You may find this hard to believe, Rebecca, but this world would be a much darker and drearier place without you in it. I'm sorry to say that Crazy Mary does not warrant the same kind of protection."

"You might think that way, Cecelia. But I don't. I can't. Crazy Mary counts just as much as you or me. No one has the right to snuff her out before the good Lord has planned. Please, help me figure out where she'll be."

Becky feared she was going to start crying. She was so tired. Part of her had to do this no matter what the risk. But there was another part of her screaming that if she'd had enough sleep and was thinking clearly, she might be agreeing with Cecelia instead of arguing with her. That scared her even more than the visions did.

"Fine," Cecelia said. "Sit."

Becky hurried and took a seat. She listened to Cecelia's voice and within seconds was in the same alley she'd dreamt about. She looked around, madly searching for something that would tip her off as to where this particular alley was. She heard Crazy Mary's cries but didn't dare look in their direction. She'd get sucked into the scene, and she didn't want to see any more than she had already. No. She needed a clue. There had to be something.

"What is around you, Rebecca?" Cecelia's voice cut through the haze of the dream.

"Bricks. Trash cans. A streetlight at either end. Nothing else! How can there be nothing else?" Becky panicked. Could it be the most nondescript alley in all of Savannah was where this murder was going to take place?

"Calm down, Becky. Calm down. Look down. Look up. Look all around you," Cecelia ordered.

Becky did as she was told and saw it. A sign that read Falls Tires and a crisscross of clotheslines with men's and women's underthings hanging from it on the fire escape. On the ground was a wooden cellar door with not just one but three padlocks on it.

"Sure. There was a gin joint down there. I remember! I know where this is!" Becky's eyes focused as she brought herself out of the trance Cecelia had helped her slip into. "I know where it is! Cecelia! It's not far from here!"

"Calm down, Becky. What do you plan on doing?"

"I'm going to stop them. Whoever it is, I'm going to get to them before they get to Crazy Mary. I have to."

Becky didn't wait for Cecelia to give her approval. Without any hesitation, Becky dashed from the apartment, down the stairs, and out the front door. Only there was she delayed when she ran smack into Nathan and Josephine Vero, who were coming in as Becky was charging out.

"My heavens, dear! What is wrong?" Mrs. Vero gasped. "You knocked the wind right out of both of us."

"I'm sorry but…" Becky started, but Nathan put his arm gently around her shoulder.

"It's all right, miss. No harm done. Why don't you come inside and have a cup of strong black tea? That'll help settle your nerves. We've even got a little blackberry jam to add to it," Mr. Vero said with a smile that pushed a million previously unseen wrinkles up around his eyes.

"I can't. I'm in a terrible hurry and…"

"What can be that important? Surely it's not life or death," Josephine said, her eyes wide and a worried grin on her face. The comment made Becky almost burst out laughing. But she didn't.

"No. My friends are waiting for me. I have to go." Becky took a step back, but the older couple was persistent and followed a step forward.

"They'll understand. Whatever has you in such a dither, I'm sure if we all put our heads together, we can come up with a solution. Is this about a specific young man, perhaps?" Josephine persisted.

"What? Uh, no. My friends are right there." Becky pointed at the car, where Teddy and Martha were looking in their direction nervously.

"Oh. We didn't realize they came with you. That's different," Nathan replied. "You youngsters go have fun, and please, come visit us and tell us how everything turned out."

"Yes sir," Becky replied. "I am sorry. I'd love a nice long visit, but… I really am terribly sorry." She waved over her shoulder as she hurried to the car and climbed in the back seat with very little regard to how much leg she was showing.

"What did the old-timers want?" Martha asked.

"They're just new people in town. I think they might be a little lonely. Teddy, remember that gin joint in the alley with the screwy password and three padlocks on the door?" Becky grabbed the shoulder of his jacket and squeezed.

"Sure do. That was the Grape Den. I think it moved and goes by a different name now. Why, toots? What's the skinny?" Teddy asked as he revved the engine.

"We have to go there. Crazy Mary is going to get killed in that same alley if I don't get there in time. Oh, golly. I'm afraid too much time has already gone by."

Becky hated that when she looked over her shoulder to see the Veros, she was angry at them for delaying her. They didn't know what she was doing. They couldn't be blamed. Still, Becky couldn't help how she felt.

"Crazy Mary? Why, she's a staple in this town! I'll do my best, Beck!" Teddy shifted gears, bulldozed his way into traffic, and hit the gas.

Becky and Martha held hands tightly as the Flivver sped down the busy streets. Teddy didn't take his hand off the horn the entire time. Finally, they came to the street they knew the alley was off of. The second the car stopped, Becky was climbing out. This part of town had people walking along the sidewalks but not many. Some were looking for an all-night poker game. Others a little company. There were straights who were actually just on their way home. Becky didn't pay attention to any of them.

"Hold on, Becky," Teddy grumbled as he got out of the car, offering his hand to Martha, who followed.

"It's down here, right?" Becky asked as she looked up and saw the crisscrosses of laundry overhead. "I remember. Yes, it's just a hop, skip, and jump from here. Down a couple paces and..."

"Becky! Don't go in there alone!" Martha hissed, trying not to attract any unwanted attention. "Teddy, she'll listen to you. Don't let her go in there."

"Beck! Wait for us!" Teddy called, but it was obvious their friend had tunnel vision. She saw nothing else but the alley and the three padlocks and the cellar door across from which Crazy Mary would have been walking. She had to have made it. Teddy broke all the rules to get here quickly. She didn't lose a second. She was sure of it.

"Becky!" Martha called. But Becky had hurried ahead of them.

"There you are!" she panted to the cellar door. "I found you! I made it. I made it. Crazy Mary should be arriving at any second and…"

Becky felt the lump in her throat before her mind even registered what it was seeing. She tried to say the word "no," but her mouth had gone dry like the white banister around her porch at high noon. What made the scene in front of her even worse was that Becky thought she'd just seen a bag of trash. But it wasn't trash. It was a person, crumpled up on the ground like that person had been discarded.

"Becky! Don't you ever run off like that to face a monster without us," Martha said, gasping as she tried to catch her breath. She smiled at her friend but quickly saw the look on Becky's face.

"What's wrong? You've gone green."

"We're too late," Becky muttered and pointed.

"If that ain't a kick in the head," Teddy whispered. He bent over the body and, with a trembling hand, pulled on her shoulder to roll her over. The body rolled over. But the head remained where it was, separated from the rest.

Martha and Becky gasped. Teddy stood up and backed away. The trio said nothing to each other as they backed out of the alley. The first person walking by was a gent in a suit.

"Hey, pal. Do me a favor," Teddy said and reached in his pocket for a nickel. "Would you call the cops? We got ourselves a serious situation here."

"What gives?" the man asked and peeked cautiously into the alley.

"You know Crazy Mary?" Teddy asked.

"Sure. Everyone knows Crazy Mary," the man replied as he touched his tie.

"Well, let's say she's cashed in. The big sleep, get me? And it wasn't no accident or act of God," Teddy added after clearing his throat.

The man looked down the alley, then back at Teddy, then to Becky and Martha, who were clinging to each other and trembling.

"Yeah, bub. I'll get the cops for ya." The man dashed across the street and down the block to an open dry cleaner. It didn't take long for the sound of sirens to fill the air, getting closer and closer.

"What are we gonna tell them?" Martha asked.

"What do you mean?" Teddy replied. "We'll tell them the truth that…"

Becky took a deep breath. "That I had a dream this was going to happen and went to a gypsy to get the details and hurried here to try to stop it? They won't fit us for nut-coats. No. A one-way ride to the loony bin. That's where we'll end up."

Martha shook her head. "No, we'll just say we were passing through. We thought the Grape Den was still open. They shouldn't think anything screwy of that?"

"Yeah, Beck," Teddy encouraged.

"But they'll know this was the same killer who has been bumping off these poor people for weeks. The same crackpot who left a body on my family's property. A body that I found," Becky said and looked down the street as the sound of sirens got closer.

Teddy looked at Martha. "This is a pickle."

"No, it isn't." Martha squared her shoulders and pointed down the street. "Becky, take a walk. Teddy and I will talk to the heat. You scram. That man went into that dry cleaner to call the police. Go wait for us there."

Becky nodded and hustled across the street. Her mind raced as she looked over her shoulder at her friends. They were good eggs. But now what was she supposed to do? She knew there was a devil out there preying on these poor, unfortunate people, but the only ones who would believe her were her friends.

Finally, she reached the dry cleaner. The bright lights inside brought her some comfort and snapped her out of the dismal reality of murder. She stepped inside and looked at the older woman behind the counter.

"I'm just dodging a masher," Becky said with an awkward grin. The woman at the counter with a row of paper-covered clothing hanging behind her was full-figured with squinty eyes and tapped a plump index finger with red polish.

"You need a drink, honey?" she asked quietly.

"Sure do," Becky replied. The woman winked and jerked her head to the left. She lifted a small section of the counter to let her pass before pulling aside a curtain of dry cleaning and revealing a slender single door.

"Go on in. The coppers aren't interested in this place," the woman said.

"I'm waiting on a couple of friends," Becky replied.

"Do you think they'd like a drink too?"

Becky chuckled. "Does a duck have a wet belly?"

"I'll send them along. We've got a couple flatfoots on the dole. No feds will be raiding tonight."

Becky was sure of that. The cops were interested in the body that was lying in the alley just a couple of doors down. Becky shivered as she turned the knob and opened the door. There was a set of concrete stairs and a red arrow pointing down where some soft music played on an old Victrola was coming from. The smell of cigar smoke brought a sense of comfort to her. The murmur of conversations and laughing eased her nerves. This was nothing more than a speakeasy. Like the dozens of other gin joints she had been to alone and with her friends, this place was normal.

No one paid any particular attention to her as she walked up to the bar. The bartender was a thin man who moved slowly but deliberately as he emptied an ashtray, poured a shot of whiskey, and lit a woman's cigarette, all in that order.

Becky stepped up and leaned against the bar. The bartender slinked over to her and leaned on the bar across from her.

"Welcome to The Clubhouse. What can I get you, chickie?" he asked, clicking his tongue and winking.

"How about three fingers of gin and a ciggy?" Becky asked. She found it funny at the moment that her father had one of the biggest tobacco plantations in Georgia and she didn't have a cigarette on her.

"Back in a flash, chickie," he said. Becky watched him pour her drink, plop in a tiny wedge of lime, and slide it down the bar to her. He pulled a cigarette from a pack on the counter behind him and returned, offering it to her, followed by a glowing match.

Becky accepted the cigarette and inhaled deeply before taking a sip of her drink. It calmed her nerves, bringing her back to the moment, the sound of the music. She remembered seeing poor Crazy Mary's body in the alley.

It's not your fault you didn't make it in time. Stop beating yourself up for it, she thought as she sipped her drink. But when she saw the movement out of the corner of her eye, she began to second-guess herself.

CHAPTER 12

The only thing Becky saw was the pair of eyes looking at her from the shadows. She sipped her drink and hoped the bitter taste would clear her vision and she'd see that she was looking at nothing more than a couple of baubles hanging from the ceiling or glints of light from a sparkling necklace or earrings. But they were eyes, wild and eager. She took a deep breath and held it.

The man who emerged from the corner wasn't like the man at the boxing match. But there was something familiar in the glow of his eyes. He approached, licked his lips, and quickly took a seat next to her.

"You're bringing them here," he said quietly.

"I think you're full of baloney. Maybe you should find a breeze," Becky said and shifted in her seat.

The man scooted closer to her. Becky could smell he hadn't had a bath in some time. As she looked at the cuff of his jacket, she saw it was frayed and stained, old and worn out from long walks and cold nights. "You're in danger."

"You don't even know me," Becky replied.

"They saw you peeping," he said. "You and the gypsy woman."

Becky looked at the man and saw his hair was combed, but his five o'clock shadow betrayed his poor financial situation.

"What?" Becky's mouth went dry. Her right eyebrow arched while she tilted her head to the right, trying to convey an attitude of disinterest. But the man once again scooted closer and leaned in. The smell of gin was heavy on his breath.

"The gypsy won't last long," he added.

"Hey, pal, why don't you ease up," the bartender interrupted. Becky had always enjoyed a visit from the bartender of any speakeasy, but at this moment she could have kissed the smooth-moving man.

"What?" the strange man asked like he didn't know what the problem could have been.

"You know this guy, chickie? I can have him

escorted to the door if you need me to," the bartender said, his eyes glued on the man.

Becky was about to take him up on his offer. But she looked at the disheveled man, and something made her change her mind.

"No. Thanks. In fact, get him a round," Becky said. "You'll join me in a drink?"

With a look of surprise on his face, like he'd been asked to solve a complex math problem, he nodded and scooted his seat a few inches away from Becky as if she'd somehow asked for a little more elbow room without saying a word.

The bartender looked the guy up and down before pouring him a shot. Becky raised her glass and toasted their health before taking a sip. The man tossed the drink back, cleared his throat and leaned on his elbows.

"You want to give me the skinny on how you know me and who is after me?" Becky asked quietly as the record player was changed to "By the Light of the Silvery Moon."

"I've seen you before," he muttered.

"Oh yeah?" Instantly Becky thought he'd slipped into some of the other clubs around town. It wasn't uncommon for her to be recognized, since she danced from the minute she entered any place to the second she left, taking a rest only to sip a cocktail and laugh with her friends.

"In my dreams," he muttered.

"If you're casting a line, buddy, I ain't bitin'." Becky snorted.

"I don't mean like that. I mean, really. I dreamed about you and those people. They're looking for you, and they won't stop until you're... one of them." He gulped. Becky watched him smooth his hair back with trembling hands.

"What people?"

"I'm not even sure if they are people. They look like people at first. Then they change." He leaned on his elbows, clenched his fists, and took a deep breath. "You've got to get out of here. You've just got to. I can't watch anymore. Miss, you need to leave town and never look back. They want what you have, and they won't stop! Do you hear me?"

"You need to pipe down, or they're going to toss you in the back of the paddy wagon," Becky ordered. The man looked around nervously before he tugged at his frayed collar.

"I warned you. I told you everything I know."

Becky shook her head. "You said you dreamed about me. Why? Why would you be having dreams about a woman you never met before?" She said this more as a question to herself instead of to this poor vagabond, who was probably so pickled after a life of drifting and drinking that he wasn't sure of his own whereabouts, let alone Becky's.

"I don't know. But I saw you. Maybe if you just stay away from the tobacco fields, you'll be all right."

"What did you just say?" Becky was about to sip her cocktail but stopped before the rim of the glass even reached her lips.

"That's where they get you. Oh, miss, just stay away from the tobacco fields. That might be enough. Yes. That's the ticket. If you stay away from there, you won't... become like they are." He swallowed hard again before he looked at Becky's half-full glass and his own empty one. She took the hint, waved to the bartender, and ordered the man another round. He gulped it down, winced as it burned his gut, then let out a sigh of relief.

How could he know about the tobacco fields?

He doesn't. It is just the ramblings of a hobo who probably suffered a bender in a tobacco field and is convinced anything associated with the plants is cursed.

But I can't avoid the tobacco fields.

Of course you can't, but half of Georgia is tobacco fields. He had a fifty-fifty chance of hitting close to home. He could have just as easily said cotton fields.

Becky's mind went round and round as she tried to reason how this man could know she lived on a tobacco plantation. For a few minutes, she just sat there and watched as this drifter seemed to have a conversation in his head. Whatever was going on in there, it had him staring ahead while he muttered

If he did know, Rebecca, he'd know you can't stay away from the tobacco fields. You live there. It's just a lucky guess. The guy's full of bunk and has gotten two drinks out of you. Now pay the tab and scram. This ain't going nowhere.

She pulled a quarter from her purse and put another next to it for the bartender to give the bum another round to keep him there while she made a clean getaway. Just as he took the shot and tossed it back, Becky hopped off her seat, mingled into the small group of couples cutting the rug, and disappeared out the back exit. Speakeasies always had a back exit just in case there was a raid. The back exit of this particular establishment was a window, but it served its purpose. No one even gave her a second look as she swung one leg over the sill and then the other.

Once out in the cool night air, Becky walked around the block just in time to catch Martha and Teddy hustling across the street toward the dry cleaners. She put her thumb and index finger in her mouth and gave a whistle that caused them both to turn.

"What happened?" Becky asked once she caught up to them.

Teddy and Martha took turns explaining the situation. When the details got to be too much for one, the other took over. The main gist of the story was that Crazy Mary was done in by the same butcher who killed several transients over the past couple of weeks.

"Did they say anything about those marks?" Becky asked.

"No. In fact, when Martha asked about them, they told us to mind our business and keep a lid on it. From the look on the flatfoot's face, he meant business," Teddy replied as he pulled Martha closer to him.

"I think we all need a drink," Martha said.

"Yeah," Becky replied half-heartedly. She didn't want to tell them about the gin joint behind the dry cleaners. Truthfully, she'd be happy to never stop in that place again. She suggested Willie's, and they all agreed. Once there, Becky felt the calming effect of her home away from home, a shared cigarette between her and Martha, and an ice-cold mint julep.

After a few minutes, the room was jumping with couples crammed on the dance floor. Becky was feeling better and added a couple of names to her dance card. Getting her body moving and her mind off the series of events and the hobo's warning was as good as a rest. Still, she worried about his warning of the tobacco fields.

"How dare he. That's my home," she muttered to herself as she walked back to Martha and Teddy, who were still discussing poor Crazy Mary. Becky pushed aside her feelings of failure. If she'd just been a few minutes earlier, just a little faster, she might have spared the broad such a gruesome end. Now it felt like half the homeless population in Savannah knew who Becky was and knew there were monsters out to get her.

As she caught her breath and took a couple of sips of gin, she felt a plan forming and, for the first time in a long time, started to feel in control.

If what the poor chum in the dry cleaner's speakeasy said was true, the killers were looking for her. Maybe it was time she got a glimpse of them. At least then they wouldn't have the advantage of anonymity anymore. Becky could hardly wait to get to sleep that night.

CHAPTER 13

*I*t was a little past midnight when Becky finally laid her head on her pillow. It wasn't hard to get Teddy and Martha to drive her home early. Although all of them needed the change in mood and atmosphere after finding poor Crazy Mary in such a state, it just seemed rather wrong to really enjoy themselves. But instead of letting the doldrums set in, Becky stealthily devised a plan. But she couldn't do it alone.

"Of course, I'll stay the night. Why, we haven't had a good old-fashioned sleepover since we were children," Martha gushed.

"And I'll make the ultimate sacrifice and stay too," Teddy offered with a wink. "I can't let anything happen to my two best girls."

"Theodore Rockdale, how dare you try to start such a scandal." Martha elbowed her best beau.

"That's right, Teddy. You'll have to play the role of humble chauffer. Bring us home and then be on your way," Becky chimed in.

"Oh, not even a nightcap for your chum Teddy?" he said, pouting.

"Not tonight," Becky said and clapped him on the back. Before leaving Willie's, they had one more round and toasted poor Crazy Mary. None of them knew anything about her other than that she'd roamed the streets of Savannah for years. Becky felt terrible that such a fate befell the bag lady, but her life wasn't all that easy as it was.

"Still. It's no excuse to snuff her out like that. She wasn't hurting anyone. None of those residents of skid row were. Just because a guy is down on his luck doesn't mean he should be easy pickings for... *that*," Teddy said as they were leaving the club to pile into the car. Becky and Martha agreed whole-heartedly.

The night had cooled down some, but there was still a stickiness in the air that made Becky feel hot and chilly at the same time. It was an uncomfortable feeling. She was shivering by the time the car pulled onto the long dirt driveway. There was still a light on in her mother's parlor and Fanny's room, where the shades were up as if it were the middle of the day. Becky and Martha both saw that first before catching Teddy.

"I've told Fanny to pull her shades down, but it's no use. She says she leaves them up because of the heat. When that excuse runs dry, she says it shouldn't matter since we are out in the middle of nowhere and no one is going to see. Why, I wouldn't be surprised if that bum found on our property hadn't gotten an eyeful just before..." Becky ran her finger across her throat as she looked at Martha.

"Well, at least he had one pleasant vision before he died," Teddy chirped.

"Teddy Rockdale, I'm going to pretend you didn't say that," Martha replied then pinched her lips together.

After coming to a stop in front of the house, Becky hopped out of the car and left the two love-birds alone for a second for Teddy to mend fences. She snuck inside the back and found her mother sitting with a book in her lap. As if by magic, Fanny appeared, wearing a shiny silk robe that she repeatedly tugged to cover her bosom.

"Are Teddy and Martha coming in?" she asked innocently, batting her eyes and flipping her hair.

"Sorry to break it to you, but only Martha. You won't get a chance to give Teddy a show. But go ahead and leave your blinds up. Someone is bound to be along eventually," Becky snapped.

"Aunt Kitty, did you hear your daughter?" Fanny gasped.

"Yes. My dear, please go pull your blinds down. I'm not sure how they do things in Paris, but here in Savannah, a lady keeps her shades drawn. Go on. Do it now," Kitty ordered then smirked at Becky. "As for you."

"Oh, Mama, please don't start. You know how she rubs me the wrong way."

"I know she does, but she's family," Kitty replied.

Becky gave up. It was no use trying to talk to her mother about Fanny. It was obvious she wasn't going to get the girl thrown out of the house at this hour, so Becky saved her breath. Fortunately, Martha came in just in time.

"Hello, Aunt Kitty," she said and hurried to give Kitty a peck on the cheek. "I hope you don't mind, but Becky invited me to stay over. I just couldn't resist. We haven't had a powwow like this in ages."

"Really? Well, I do hope you'll make your cousin Fanny feel a part of things. She is a guest in our home, after all," Kitty said smoothly.

"Of course we will, Kitty. I know that Becky wouldn't have it any other way. In fact, she actually said that it just wasn't the same without Fanny there," Martha sang like a canary. Even though almost everything out of her mouth was bunk, Becky saw how it did make her mother happy. She let it go. The truth was it wasn't the same without Fanny. It was a relaxed and enjoyable time, the gruesome death of one of Savannah's most notorious transients notwithstanding.

"That does my heart good to hear," Kitty replied.

"Gadzooks," Becky said as she yawned. "It's getting late. We better get upstairs and find you a decent pair of pajamas. Good night, Mama." Becky grabbed Martha's hand before her best friend could sink her in any deeper with the yarns about missing Fanny.

"Good night, girls," Kitty said before going back to her book.

"Did you have to lay it on so thick?" Becky whispered as they went upstairs.

"I couldn't help it. Once the words started coming out of my mouth, they just wouldn't stop. Hey, look what Teddy gave me." She pulled a flask from a secret pocket on the inside of her dress.

"What a good egg," Becky tittered.

"What's that you got there?" Fanny asked as she pulled her bedroom door open.

"None of your beeswax," Becky replied.

"It's a little gin. Want a snort?" Martha replied.

"Bathtub gin? I really am more accustomed to champagne. But when in Rome." Fanny tugged at her robe and followed the girls into Becky's bedroom.

"So, what's the real plan?" Martha asked as they shut the door and Martha handed Fanny the flask.

"I need you to watch me sleep," Becky replied.

"You're out of your gourd. What for?" Martha asked before taking the flask from Fanny before the blonde drank it all.

"I'm going to have my sketchbook, and I need to draw what I dream. You have to help me do that," Becky replied as she started to unbutton her dress.

"You should at least stand behind your changing screen," Fanny said. "All the ladies in Paris, no matter if it was their own mother in the room, always stood behind a changing screen when disrobing."

"Fanny, sometimes you can be a real bluenose," Martha replied as she began to unbutton her own dress. "Now make yourself useful and help me get the buttons in the middle. I can't reach."

"I just know I'll see them tonight," Becky said. "It's a feeling in my gut. So when you see I've fallen asleep, just make sure I keep my pencil in my hand and the paper on my lap," Becky said, standing there in her simple white silk underthings. Martha's were almost identical except for the tiny pink MB stitched at the hem of her camisole.

"You should see the things Becky has in her sketchbook," Fanny said with a slight slur.

"Hey, don't hog the hooch," Martha said and snatched the flask away before Fanny could take another gulp.

"They are the obscenest things I've ever seen," Fanny added before sitting down on the hope chest at the end of Becky's bed and looking around the room. "I never realized how dark it is in here. You really should try to lighten things up, Rebecca. It looks like a funeral parlor."

"Would you shut up for one second?" Becky shook her head. "Can you do that for me?" She looked at Martha, who shrugged, took the flask from Fanny, and handed it to Becky, who took a quick sip.

Martha pushed her hair away from her forehead. "I better not have any of this, then, or I'll be sawing logs before either one of you doze off. Then who will break up the inevitable catfight between you two?" She chuckled.

Fanny continued to mutter to herself as she

looked around Becky's room, studying each collected feather, pebble, and scrap of fabric. Neither Becky nor Martha paid her too much attention but instead stretched out on Becky's four-poster bed and turned the oil lamp on the nightstand down so the room was barely lit.

"So, just stay awake and watch you sleep?" Martha asked as she began to flip through a book she'd found on Becky's desk. She was sitting up, her feet stretched out in front of her and her back propped up against the headboard.

"Yes," Becky replied as she took a couple of deep breaths. "I'm not actually going to sleep. I'm going into a sort of trance."

"A trance? Beck, is that safe?" Martha asked.

"When I was in Paris with Grandma Louise, I was quite the pupil of all things occult. Trances. Séances. Fortune-telling. I was told more than once that I had a keen sense of the spirit world." Fanny yawned before standing up and flipping her hair. "Rebecca, your little trick sounds rather juvenile. But then again, you always were the child in the family who got dirtiest and took the most foolhardy risks. I guess some things never change."

"Are you staying? Because if you are, you need to pipe down and go to sleep," Becky whispered.

"Where would I sleep?" Fanny huffed.

"There is plenty of room on the floor," Becky replied with a smirk.

"We can scooch over," Martha said, trying to keep the peace. "There's room in the bed for the three of us. Why, my twin cousins from Odell must weigh at least five hundred pounds combined, and all three of us squeezed onto two army cots wired together and slept just fine. Plus, I'm not even going to be sleeping. I'm going to be staring at Becky all night long, waiting for her to fall asleep. See? It's all ducky."

"Yeah, ducky," Becky huffed as she punched her pillow and let her head fall into it.

"Thank you very much, but I'm not accustomed to cramming into bed like sardines in a can," Fanny replied and yawned again. "You two have fun. I'll be stretched out comfortably in my bed. Toodle-oo." Becky and Martha looked at each other and rolled their eyes as Fanny pulled the door shut.

"You know, Martha, I thought I was going to be too nervous to sleep, but after dealing with my bubble-headed cousin, I am utterly exhausted."

"Becky, you said you were going into a trance. That's not sleeping. That's something different. What if you get stuck there? What if I can't snap you out of it?" Martha asked.

"You won't have to worry. I was able to snap myself out of it with Cecelia. No reason I can't do it again," Becky replied with a confident smile.

"I don't know about this."

"It'll be a cakewalk. I promise." Becky propped up her pillow against the headboard and made sure her sketchbook was open to a blank page and her pencil poised in her hand.

Although she was sure she could recreate Madame Cecelia's calming instructions to slip into the trance, she wasn't sure what she was supposed to look for once she got there. And Martha did pose an interesting problem. Even if she did find what she was looking for, what if she couldn't snap herself out of it? She'd be stuck in a place in between wakefulness and sleep. That could be a very scary place.

"Okay, if you say so," Martha replied and focused on the book she'd picked up. Becky relaxed her body and began to focus on where she saw Crazy Mary. She recalled the poor bum that was found on her family's property. There had to be something there between them that tied the two victims to their attackers.

It didn't happen all at once, but piece by piece, Becky was slipping the puzzle pieces together. She felt as light as air as her hand flew across her sketchbook pages while her eyes studied figures and shapes and shadows.

Finally, something came into focus that was familiar to her. A striped wall. Two of them. Dozens of them. Fuzzy things in rows. Crazy music that was off-key. Lots of people. Some were talking while others were laughing. It didn't sound like a lonely place or a place where there would be a death. Finally, the vision slipped into crystal-clear view, and Becky sighed.

"The carnival," she whispered, unsure if she spoke out loud or if it was all in her head. Now she scanned the scenery. What she was looking for was still a mystery. Was this the place the killer was —or killers were—going to strike again? How would she know who it was?

It isn't like dabbling in the future-reading business is easy or even reliable, her meddling conscience said. *What if you see something you don't want to or aren't supposed to? This isn't right or fair. Life is supposed to unfold naturally.*

"But Cecelia says it's a gift. And I'm not using it for some flim-flam. I'm trying to stop a killer," she replied, again unsure if it was out loud or in her head.

Just as she was about to continue her argument

with herself, she saw something she wasn't prepared for. It was the Veros. They were shuffling along through the crowds of people, just minding their own business.

"No," Becky replied. But she was helpless to stop the image that ran like a moving picture in front of her. She watched as they walked slowly like two older people would, Mrs. Vero with her arm linked tightly through the crux of Mr. Vero's elbow.

"This isn't fair. They aren't transients. They're just old. They can't possibly be the next victims. They just can't," Becky mumbled. Still, she followed them as they wove their way through the people, oblivious they were being watched. It didn't take long.

Becky felt her hand moving across the page of her sketchbook but had no control over what it was drawing. In her vision, she followed the couple as they made their way deeper inside the carnival. There was a flash, and she saw them venture between two tents. Why would they do that? Why would they slip out of view like that? Didn't they know it was dangerous to go between the booths and tents? Shady characters sometimes snuck around those places looking to pick someone's pocket or worse.

That was when Becky saw him. His movements looked suspicious. He jerked his head to the left and the right and walked like he had tied one on earlier and was just getting his balance back. Unfortunately, Becky couldn't get a straight-on view of him. His hair was a dirty blond and thinning in the back. A round circle of skin was starting to show on his crown.

Then, like with most dreams, a small sliver made sense, but that never lasted very long. Suddenly things became as strange and distorted as any mirror in a funhouse. Becky could no longer see clearly. Everything was bent and shadowed, and even though she knew she was still at the carnival, it had become a strange, dark place. Her footsteps became heavy, like she had weights around her ankles while she was trying to trudge through mud. She opened her mouth to call out, but barely a whisper could be heard.

Finally, as she was about to peek around the corner down between two attraction tents and get a clear look at the man who had followed the poor unsuspecting Veros, she instead found herself nose to nose with something else.

Nothing but a set of red eyes glared at her from the darkness.

"There you are." She heard those words as if whatever it was whispered directly into her ear while staring into her face. Did its lips stretch that far? Had it pulled her ear toward its cruel mouth?

"There you aaarrrreeee," it hissed again. Becky turned to run away, scrambling, desperately trying to pull her weak legs from the invisible putty they were getting stuck in and dash away from those eyes. It was like everything was happening in slow motion. Still, her voice was gone, and even though she was trying to scream, nothing more than a pitiful grunt came from her lips. Her lungs just wouldn't fill up enough for her to belt out a real call for help. Her arms were exhausted, and with one final burst, she mustered up every bit of strength she could and gave her right leg a yank.

Suddenly she was wide awake, face down on her wooden floor, having fallen right out of bed.

"Becky? Are you all right?" It was Martha. Becky held still for a few seconds while seeing the familiar comforts of her room wrapped around her like a blanket. There was a pain in the meaty flesh of her hand. When she opened her fist, she saw the broken ends of her pencil digging into her palm. She'd cracked it in two.

"Yeah, I'm just ducky," Becky said and took a few gulps of air.

"You had me scared out of my skin. I was just a second away from calling Aunt Kitty," Martha said as she reached down from the side of the bed and helped her friend to her feet.

"I'm glad you didn't. My sketchbook? Where is it?" Becky looked around her feet but didn't see it.

"It's right here. But Becky, you might not want to look at it," Martha said, holding the book like she might hug a pillow.

"Why? It was the whole point of going through this... nightmare, to see what I could see. Hand it over or you'll be wearing a Chicago overcoat before sunup," Becky joked.

Martha didn't crack even the slightest grin as she reluctantly handed over the book.

At first, Becky didn't remember her dream. She flipped past the pages of doodles and rough sketches of the Old Brick Cemetery. Past the gruesome images that had been coming to her on a regular basis, depicting the fates of those poor souls who wandered the streets of Savannah. Finally, she stopped and looked intently at what she'd drawn while she was asleep. A shiver ran up her spine, making her cold, even though the sheer curtains across her windows barely moved.

"Becky, what is all this?" Martha asked.

Becky swallowed hard. Her mouth had instantly gone dry. She looked at the book. Her nightmare came rushing back. The carnival. The space between the tents. The Veros. And that man with the bald spot. Her hands trembled as she flipped the pages. They looked like nothing more than terrifying, haunting scribbles to Martha, but Becky knew what she was trying to draw. She knew what she had seen. The last page was nothing but darkness. Black scribbles, pressed hard into the paper, around two glaring eyeballs. Becky clapped the book shut. She was afraid those eyes she drew might be able to see into her room.

"You and Teddy want to go to the carnival tomorrow?"

Martha looked at Becky and put her hand against her best friend's forehead.

"Rebecca Madeline? Are you feeling okay?"

Becky chuckled but didn't answer. She had a nervous feeling in her gut and decided the first chance she got, she was going to burn that sketchbook.

CHAPTER 14

Under the bright beautiful sun, which shone without a cloud in the sky, Becky could almost feel brave about her plan to go to the carnival and look for Mr. and Mrs. Vero. She didn't have to tell Martha what she'd gathered from her dream. Unlike most nonsense dreams that dissolved under the weight of wakefulness, Becky's dream followed her from her room, downstairs, and out onto the porch, where she sat with Martha, sipping coffee and eating Lucretia's honey buns.

"I'm just afraid that those poor folks who just immigrated here are this maniac's next bullseye," Becky said. "It's not a difficult plan."

"Right. There will just be half of Savannah in attendance. Even the chance of rain won't keep people away," Martha huffed. "Why can't we just go warn them and tell them not to come?"

Becky sighed. "Because we won't be able to catch the monster who's been doing this. We have to let things play out like in my dream and then catch the guy in the act. Well, before he starts the act, I hope. You know what I mean. Wait. Did you just say there's a chance of rain tonight?"

"Yes. Before I came over here yesterday, I was chatting with Aunt Rue. She'd stopped by our house to let my mother know about a recipe Mama had been hunting for." Martha waved her hand as if shooing a fly. "Anyhoo, she was complaining about the ache in her knees, and everyone knows Aunt Rue's achy knees are a better weather indicator than those balloons they send up in the air, which do next to nothing, as far as I can see."

"Oh. How reliable are Aunt Rue's knees?" Becky asked.

"According to her, they are never wrong. Just like she never is." Martha giggled.

Aunt Rue was a staple among the upper crust of people in Savannah. Although she looked like she'd spent a good amount of time on the street in line for a room at the local shelter, she was a wealthy woman with a good head on her shoulders and heart of gold behind her huge bosom. Often, there was an unusually strong drink in her hand too. Friend to banker and bootlegger alike, Aunt Rue was a fountain of information but managed to dole it out only when necessary. Becky always liked her and thought if she was going to ever grow up, she'd like to grow up to be like Aunt Rue. Without a care to what anyone thought, who did kindnesses on the sly and who might look poor but was rich not just with money but common sense and good friends.

Becky had helped her when she was worried her gardener John was thinking of leaving her. Becky had heard stories spread about Aunt Rue and John's relationship. Of course, the people of Savannah, whether they cared to admit it or not, loved the seedy side of things, even if they had to conjure it up themselves. The truth was that John and Aunt Rue were the best of friends, like brother and sister. It was a simple misunderstanding that Becky had seen played out and discussed at length with the spirits that walked around town. She didn't dare tell Aunt Rue how she found out what John's problem was. But she always had the feeling Aunt Rue knew more than she was letting on. The woman always did. She and John had mended fences, and he was still her gardener, much to the rest of Savannah's chagrin. Aunt Rue always won the blue ribbon for her flowers and vegetables at the annual county fair.

"So, it's going to rain tomorrow. In the morning or at night? Will we get a thunderstorm or just some sprinkles? It's a perfectly beautiful day today. Hot but still lovely nonetheless, and I think tomorrow should be..."

"Becky, I don't know the answer to that. All I know is Aunt Rue says her legs told her it was going to rain. And she believes her legs," Martha said. "But even if there is a torrential downpour, you know you can count on Teddy and me. We'd love to go with you."

"Go with you? Where are you two off to this time?" Fanny asked, making Becky gasp in surprise.

"You mean you weren't listening to the whole conversation from the screen door?" Becky muttered. "I'm shocked."

"What was that, Rebecca?" Fanny asked, batting her long lashes as she slipped onto the swing next to Martha and looked at Becky head-on.

Martha replied politely, "Uh... we're going to the carnival tonight. You know, the one that popped up at the end of your property down the dirt path. We were all going to walk. Just didn't seem like the sort of thing you would be interested in, Fanny." Martha took a sip of her coffee.

"You're going to hike down the path? In this heat?" Fanny put her hand up to her neck. Her red-painted nails stood out against her pale creamy skin. Becky had freckles all over. Adam had told her he loved them. Why he popped into her head at this moment she didn't know, but she quickly pushed the thought of him aside.

"We're going tonight. It might rain," Becky replied. "You probably won't want to go if it's going to rain."

"I didn't hear anyone mention rain. In fact, Aunt Kitty was just talking to Uncle Judge about how lovely it would be to sit on the porch under the full moon tonight," Fanny replied. "I think a stroll in the evening would be delightful. Is anyone else coming along?"

Just as Fanny asked to tag along, Becky recognized the sound of the Flivver coming up the driveway. A smile spread across her face as she stood and walked to the edge of the porch. Sure enough, the shiny Ford with the portly driver wearing goggles quickly approached. Becky waved. Herbert honked the horn in return.

"What's the time, catnip?" Herbert barked as he

heaved himself out from behind the wheel before grabbing a bouquet of flowers from the passenger seat.

"Now this is a pleasant surprise," Becky replied and smoothed her skirt, unable to stop smiling. Herbert walked up to the porch steps, propped one foot on the bottom step, and presented her the flowers.

"Why, Mr. Coleman. No one said you'd be stopping by," Fanny purred as she perched on the edge of the swing. "I'd have put on a nicer dress."

Becky rolled her eyes.

"Hello, Fanny. Miss Martha. Nice to see you. I didn't send word of my arrival. Plus, I'm here to see Miss Rebecca," Herbert said with a wink. "So, tell me, Becky. Have you got room on your dance card for me tonight?"

Becky smiled, and just as she was about to speak, Fanny chimed in. "Becky and Martha and I are walking to the carnival just a hop, skip, and jump from here. I'm sure Becky would love to have you join us."

Becky looked at Herbert with a sly grin. She couldn't help but feel light in her heart when Herbert was there. He wasn't anything like she was used to. Boisterous, flashy, and loud, Herbert made

Becky feel like she deserved to get the attention that only someone like Fanny would get.

"What do you say, kitten? Mind if I join the gang?" he asked.

"That would be ducky."

"But we aren't going to walk. I'll drive," he insisted.

"Oh, thank goodness. I was just telling Becky that walking down the path would have been a bad idea, especially in this heat, and we'd all be such a sweaty mess by the time we arrived," Fanny chimed in.

"If you say so," Becky cooed before taking a sniff of her flowers while still peeking over the blooms at Herbert.

"Why, Herbert Coleman. This is a nice surprise," Kitty said as she came out on the porch. "Becky's father is inside. I know he'd just love to have a chat with you."

"Greetings, Mrs. MacKenzie. I'd love a chance to chew the fat with Mr. MacKenzie. Excuse me, ladies. Rebecca," Herbert said as he wiped his forehead with a kerchief he pulled from his pocket then climbed the porch steps and headed inside.

It took just a few minutes before Becky could hear her father laughing loudly at something

Herbert had said. It warmed her heart to hear Judge having a good time with Herbert.

"My goodness, Judge does seem to get on with Herbert. How are things going with him, dear?" Kitty asked as she inspected the leaves of a potted plant next to her wicker chair. Becky pinched her lips together tightly as she watched her mother gloat, as much as Kitty MacKenzie would.

"He's all right. I wouldn't toss him to the dogs yet," Becky replied casually.

"Aunt Kitty, he's driving us all to the carnival tonight. Maybe Becky will manage to stay out of trouble if he's there," Fanny said. "Speaking of which. Martha, did Becky draw anything interesting last night?"

Becky glared at her cousin. Had her mother not been there, she would have pulled out every blond hair on her head.

"Yes. She drew a beautiful sketch of her desk as well as a butterfly that looks as if it could fly right off the page. She really does have a talent, Aunt Kitty. Not many people can do what she does," Martha said casually.

Fanny folded her arms in front of her, obviously annoyed that her attempt to get Becky behind the eight ball failed, thanks to Martha. Because of that, the conversation stayed light, and before Becky knew it, everyone was planning on staying or returning for dinner that evening. It made the wait for their trip to the carnival much more tolerable, and as Becky helped Lucretia and Kitty bring out the fried chicken and cornbread to the picnic table in the backyard, there wasn't a cloud in the sky.

CHAPTER 15

When Teddy arrived just as dinner was being served, Becky could have been knocked down with a feather by the vision she saw.

"Who is that riding with Theodore? I swear, that boy knows too many people," Martha replied as she stood to go and greet her beau with a peck on the cheek.

Becky followed. It didn't take long for her to see who it was, and a smile spread across her face. There were few things that brought such pleasure to the heart as seeing an old friend after a long hiatus.

"Well, well, well, look what the cat dragged in," Becky squawked. "I must say, Stephen Penbroke, you do get handsomer every time I see you. How was your trip to New York? I was sure those city slickers were going to hog-tie you and keep you there."

"Miss Rebecca MacKenzie, you sure are a rose among thorns. Do you really think those cosmopolitan types could keep me from here? From you?" Stephen said as he climbed out of the car, and he scooped Becky up then twirled her around.

"I know everyone will be thrilled to see you." Becky squeezed him around the neck before taking him by the hand and leading him to the front porch.

"What am I? Chopped liver?" Teddy asked.

Martha gave Stephen a quick peck on the cheek. "Oh, you know you're the cat's pajamas. There's lemonade for you too," she chirped.

"Whose jalopy is that?" Stephen asked, pointing at the other Ford in the driveway.

"That bus belongs to Mr. Herbert Coleman. My mother thought he'd make a perfectly fine suitor for me," Becky replied with a smile.

"Oh. Do you agree with her?" It was a well-known fact that Stephen Penbroke was interested in Becky MacKenzie. His attempts to woo her were of no secret to anyone. However, patience was his strategy. Stephen seemed content to wait out all others, as if he knew they'd all cheese it like Adam had or be given the bum's rush like all the others.

"He's really swell, Stephen. I gotta say I think you'll see he's running on all cylinders. A good egg," Becky said.

"If you like him, he's all right in my book. And may the best man win," Stephen replied with a sly grin and a raise of his chin.

Herbert was just as cordial to Stephen as he was to Teddy, although he had claimed to have a severe jealous streak where Becky was concerned. She was glad. The last thing she needed was for the men in her life to put on an embarrassing display of masculinity by seeing who could spit the farthest.

In fact, the men got along so well and told such fish tales around the picnic table that Becky had almost forgotten about her plan for the evening and what she was actually setting out to do later that evening.

You're chasing down the person who's been killing the destitute of this town. Just because you have a roof over your head doesn't mean he won't kill you too. Or worse, one of your friends, Becky's conscience needled as she watched the sun begin to slip behind the long rows of tobacco.

Everyone was coming with. It was a regular New Year's Eve party accompanying her on this search.

Everyone would be keeping their eyes out for Mr. and Mrs. Vero.

"Once we find them, we just follow them. They are old and unfamiliar with things yet. I don't think it would be wise to tell them we think a killer is going to strike and they were the patsies. One of them could have a grabber right in front of us," Becky instructed her friends as they collected themselves and got ready to walk the path to the carnival.

"I'm on board with everything you said, kitten," Herbert said. "But one thing. Why do we have to walk?"

Becky looked at Stephen, Martha, Teddy, and Fanny, who yawned and fanned her face.

"We don't have to, I suppose. I just thought it would be a nice night for it. The air smells so good, and the lightning bugs are just floating along on the tiniest breeze," she replied.

"I'm with Herbert," Fanny chirped. "Walking along that dirty path is no way for ladies our age to get anywhere. I say we take Herbert's Flivver. I do just love the way it sparkles in the moonlight."

"How about it, sweetheart? You don't want to snag those pretty stockings on the brambles and briars, do you?" Herbert peeked at Becky over his cheeks, which were puffed from the smirk on his lips.

"Oh, you don't have to worry about that. Becky couldn't keep the runs from her pantyhose if her life depended on it," Fanny gushed then tittered. "You'd think someone stretched them over a couple of baseball bats instead of legs."

"We'll walk with you, Becky," Martha said. "I think it's a lovely night to take a stroll. Just like when we were kids and would sneak out, collect Theodore, and play ghost-in-the-graveyard. Oh, we did have ourselves a time."

"I'm not sure where we're headed, but Herbert, if you don't mind me tagging along, I'd prefer to drive," Stephen said. "I felt like I walked all over Manhattan while I was there and would like to save my strength for pounding the pavement of the carnival, not the uneven dirt path that crosses over Memory Lane."

Becky was a little disappointed in him *and* Herbert. But rather than scold either one of them, she just smiled and shrugged her shoulders. "Suit yourselves."

"This is turning out to be a wonderful evening," Fanny said. "I'm being escorted to the carnival by two such handsome gentlemen. It reminds me so much of my time in Paris when I barely left the flat without a new chaperone to accompany me. Although Grandma Louise never picked out any men as fine as you two boys." Fanny slipped one arm through Herbert's and the other through Stephen's.

Becky, Martha, and Teddy walked past Herbert's Flivver but not before Herbert took Becky's hand. "I promise when we get there to win you a Kewpie doll," he said and kissed her cheek. When she saw the look of annoyance on her cousin's face, Becky smiled and nodded but said nothing more.

Martha had been right. The stroll down the path was just like when they were kids.

"Minus the memory of the poor sap who nearly lost his head," Teddy said. "Come on, let's make tracks. I've got a hankering for some cotton candy and a hot dog."

"We aren't going to the carnival for the carnival. We're going to catch the creeper who's been bumping off all the residents of skid row. If we can catch Mr. and Mrs. Vero heading into the place, then maybe, if we follow them, they'll lead us right to the sicko."

"Are you sure it's those old-timers?" Teddy asked.

"Hey, fate spun the bottle and it landed on them. I can't help what I saw. But I saw it, and now we're going to at least get a good look at the killer," Becky replied. She and Martha took turns telling Teddy the details of the dream and the drawings and what they were sure they were going to stop from taking place.

"I didn't make it for Crazy Mary. I can't let him get away with it again." Becky pulled her shoulders around her ears as if to protect herself from the chill of failure.

"It isn't your fault, Becky," Teddy said. "You tried the best you could. What do you expect? You've got some weird gift of being able to see things. But let's face the facts. You aren't supposed to have that gift. There is no instruction manual. And to be frank, it's a little weird how we get in these pickles with you."

"I'm sorry. I shouldn't have asked you all to come," Becky started.

"Applesauce. How much drinking and dancing can one person stand before they want to shake things up a bit? I don't know about Theodore, but I wouldn't have it any other way." Martha took Becky's hand like when they were little girls.

"And how," Teddy chimed in.

"You guys are top drawer. Really the cream of the crop," Becky said.

When they reached the entrance of the carnival, a clown with bright-red lips and a pointed yellow hat took their money in exchange for tickets. Everyone within a twenty-mile radius was there. It sounded so much like what Becky had heard in her dream that she almost lost her balance. The same laughing, the same squealing, the same muffled conversations.

"It's going to happen," Becky said.

As soon as the words left her mouth, a cool breeze blew over her. She looked up in time to see a thin strip of clouds cross the moon. Off in the distance was a flash that looked like lightning. The rain was on its way.

CHAPTER 16

"One of us should go and see if Herbert has arrived. He probably had to park in the next county. Look at all that commotion," Teddy said as they surveyed the cars lined up and parked in the huge field. People of all sorts hurried up and bought their tickets to enter the grounds. If any of them had heard rain was coming, it didn't deter them in the slightest.

Becky wasn't looking for Herbert. She was keeping her eyes peeled for two helpless older people in shabby clothes with heavy accents who just arrived in America to start a new life. They were a couple of chumps. Easy pickings for this madman. But Becky was determined to find them first.

The minutes ticked by. Becky paced a few steps

to the left and then the right, all the while keeping her eyes on the booth with the clown where people entered the grounds. She didn't see the Veros yet. But she spotted Fanny. It was impossible to miss her. She was clinging to Stephen and Herbert like she'd been tossed off the *Titanic* and they were life preservers.

Had Becky been out on any other night, her temper would have bubbled over, and she would have given Fanny a sock in the chops the way she was hanging on the boys, especially Herbert. He'd been such a good egg, and even though he wore a spare tire, he was the kind of man a girl could get used to. Someone who would show her a good time and be grateful for her. Still, as much as she wanted to move on from Adam, as much as she never wanted to feel that kind of pain of rejection again, she was always hoping to catch a glimpse of him wherever she was. Now was no different. She couldn't even say for sure that she'd be able to stay angry with him for stepping out on her. That scared her almost as much as trying to find this madman before he could hurt the Veros.

"I'll be right back." Teddy took Martha by the hand.

"Where are you going?" Becky asked.

"Delilah and Zachary are over there at the strongman bell." Teddy pointed. Just a few paces behind the clown at the ticket booth was a tall yellow plank with a bell at the top. Swing down the mallet hard enough to ring the bell, and you could win your sweetie a prize.

"Oh, yeah. I almost didn't recognize them, since they weren't necking." Becky chortled.

"He owes me a fin. I'm going to go see if I can collect. Come on, doll," Teddy said while pulling Martha along with him. "We'll be back in a flash."

Becky nodded absently, too caught up in her own thoughts to realize she was being left alone. Fanny and the boys had drifted into the carnival crowd. She tried to spy them, but it was no use. The thought of leaving the entrance to find them and risk missing the Veros kept her pacing the same five steps back and forth.

But as the night went on and the flashes of lightning got closer and closer, more of the carnival-goers began heading back to their cars or bicycles or walking out of the grounds in their direction of home.

Maybe your dream was wrong. Maybe you've thrown a wrench into the works by even being here. Maybe the culprit dreamt of you, too, and changed his plans. Becky's thoughts were relentless. She swallowed hard and wondered what her next step should be.

Your next step should be in the direction Martha and Teddy headed, and then turn and head toward the nearest speakeasy to forget your troubles. That's what your next step should be. Why do you care so much? This isn't your concern. These people aren't kin. Just go inside the carnival, get a kisser full of cotton candy and a sip of root beer before it starts raining, and maybe you can salvage some of the evening if Fanny hasn't dug her claws too deep into Herbert or Stephen.

With a deep sigh, Becky decided she'd had enough. She'd done her best and searched for the old couple. They were either in the carnival already or, if what she saw in her dream was true, maybe they were already dead. That thought made her shiver. Still, there was nothing more she could do except find her friends and Fanny and make the best of the night.

She made her way deeper and deeper into the festivities, past ring-toss games and guess-the-weight attractions, past the merry-go-round and taffy-pulls, with still no sight of her friends. Finally, when she was about to give up and head back to the path and make her way home, she saw him.

It wasn't Teddy or Herbert or even Adam, who

she'd wished would appear from around a corner but never did. It was the man with the budding bald spot and shabby suit. It was straight out of her dream, the drawing she scribbled. It was him. She was sure of it. And had she not known who he was, she might not have noticed his nervous behavior or jittery, jerky movements as he kept looking over his shoulder, first to the left and then to the right.

For a split second, Becky froze. Should she follow him? By herself? Without the help of the gang? There was safety in numbers, after all.

If she didn't move, she was going to lose him. If nothing else, she needed to get a good description of the man so when tomorrow's news listed the Veros as victims, at least she'd be able to remember the guy's mug.

Quickly, she hurried to close the gap between them. Making sure she didn't give herself away, she ducked behind strolling couples and wooden clap-boards advertising Lydia the Tattooed Lady or Hit the Bullseye and Win a Prize.

While she crept behind him, she also scanned the crowd for her friends. Even Fanny would be better than no one. But she was alone. As if that wasn't bad enough, she felt a drop hit her forehead. It was starting to rain. Just a couple of drops. Nothing to be concerned about. There wasn't any lightning in the sky. The temperature hadn't dropped any further. She had plenty of time.

Just then, the man did what Becky had hoped he wouldn't. He stopped at an opening between two tents. There was a display for the first tent of a world-famous goat named Sally that had five legs. The other tent housed a man who was over six and a half feet tall.

Carefully, Becky inched her way to the entrance between the two tents, weaving her way through people all seeming to stroll in the opposite direction, slowing her down. Finally, she made it to the space between the two tents. The wind kicked up, causing the heavy material to wave just enough to obstruct her view. Over the carnival music and people's chatter, she couldn't hear anything. Her only option was to walk between the tents.

They are helpless old people, she told herself. *If you don't help them, who will? The chances of this guy going through with the killing once you've seen him will be slim and none, and Slim left town.* It was true. She was their only hope. Carefully, she stepped between the tents. Even though the air was heavy in the small space separating each attraction, Becky trembled. Up ahead was the shadow of the man she'd been following. Where was he going? What could he be thinking as he marched down the corridor? The smell of stale popcorn and urine from anyone who couldn't find a bathroom was almost unbearable.

Just as Becky was sure the man was going to exit the other side and get lost in the crowd, she saw him stop. Instinctively, she held her breath and froze like a rabbit. The only thing giving off any light was the glow from inside the attractions on either side. It made the man look like his arms and legs were bleeding into the shadows.

"Stop right there," he hissed. Becky strained to see who he was speaking to.

"We had an agreement. You can't do this now." The accent was familiar. It was Mrs. Vero. She was on the other side of the man.

Squatting down, Becky tried to peer through the man's legs to get an idea of where the woman was. If she could give this man a shove, maybe Mrs. Vero would have a chance to get away. Becky too.

As she got down on the ground, she thought of Fanny's comment about her nylon stockings. There went another pair out the window. Oh, how she hated when Fanny was right. Creeping forward like a scolded pup might sneak to the dinner table, Becky looked through the man's legs to see the hem of Mrs.

Vero's dress and her thick ankles and bare feet. Bare feet? Behind her was another set of bare feet poking out from a pair of trousers that had to belong to Mr. Vero.

"No. This wasn't part of the deal. I won't do it," the man blubbered. He didn't sound like a man getting the jump on a couple of helpless immigrants. He sounded scared. But what could he possibly be scared of? They couldn't strong-arm him into anything. Not in their advanced years.

"You will. Or else you'll end up like the others," Mrs. Vero said in a singsong way.

"I didn't agree to any of this. You and your husband are crazy. Off your nut is what you are." The man was about to turn. If he did, he'd trip right over Becky like she'd planned. But that didn't happen. Something took a hold of him.

"If you won't give it to us, we'll just take it from you." Mrs. Vero's voice cracked.

Becky had seen it all wrong. Her dream wasn't of this man hunting down the Veros. It was the other way around.

Just as Becky was about to stand up and demand to know what kind of extortion was going on, she saw a transformation that made her limbs go numb.

Still looking between the poor man's legs at the

Veros' bare feet, Becky was sure there was a reasonable explanation for why they didn't have any shoes and that there was no time to focus on it when someone was going to get their comeuppance.

"No! You won't!" The man turned to run, and when he did, he stomped his size-twelve clodhopper right on Becky's hand. She let out a howl. He let out a yelp as he instantly jumped back, losing his balance. The shadows and light played tricks on Becky, making it look like the Veros had suddenly sprouted another set of arms or maybe tentacles. She stared up only to see a long writhing thing slither inside the bum's old shirt and pull him tight to Mr. Vero. The man went rigid with pain. With his last breath, the man was about to scream, but his mouth was covered by another appendage. Or at least that was what it looked like. Becky's mind raced to explain what she was looking at. Motivated by shock and terror, she started to scramble backward.

"Where do you think you are going, Rebecca? Isn't this what you wanted? To find us? Here we are." Mr. Vero leaned forward, the limp body of the homeless man still in what should have been Mr. Vero's arms but instead were strange, slick things.

"You—you're the ones. You've been killing these

poor people," Becky managed to stammer, even though her mouth was dry.

"They agree to give us what we need. Strange how they always change their mind when the rent is due," Mr. Vero said from an evil grimace.

"What is it th-that you need?" Becky stammered.

"Just their blood." Mr. Vero laughed.

"And what do you want with me?" she asked, feeling the burning of tears in her eyes.

"You? Why, your sight, of course. You will help us stay one step ahead of the law," Mr. Vero said.

He was doing a lot of talking, which was unusual, since it was Mrs. Vero who chatted her up during the daytime. A crack of lightning shot across the sky, followed by booming thunder. Heaven opened, and the rain began to fall.

"I won't help you at all. No, sir, I'd rather die than help you... you... monsters," Becky replied, but her voice cracked and gave away her fear.

"Oh, you'll help us. Yes, you will."

Becky looked past Mr. Vero to a skulking form that slowly started to get bigger and bigger like a cow deciding it had had enough walking on four legs and would rise and walk on two. Becky screamed as loud as she could. To her, it barely came out. The rain and the people running to their cars and down the paths out of the carnival easily drowned out any sound she could have made. The drops came down steadily and managed to snake their way down Becky's back. Or was it those strange tethers she saw spreading out from Mr. Vero? Or was it something she hadn't seen yet coming from Mrs. Vero?

"Becky! Is that you?" The voice came from behind her.

"Herbert!" Becky shouted.

Before she could get to her feet, Mr. Vero shrank back to his original size, retracting his shadowy appendages after tossing the limp body of the bum right into Becky. She fell back, bumping her head on the ground. The weight of the lifeless man was too much for her to quickly wriggle out from. She pushed and pulled, trying to kick and roll away from the body.

"What in tarnation is going on here?" Herbert yelled.

"That's what we'd like to know." Just then from behind Mrs. Vero appeared two men who looked like they'd been riding the rails for years and sipping from bottles wrapped in paper bags. It was like they didn't even see the Veros, who glared at Herbert and then Becky before shuffling in the other direction out of the narrow shaft between the two tents.

"It's like they don't even see them," Becky muttered. "Stop them! The Veros! Stop those people!"

"Looks to me like these two had some kind of flim-flam going to rob those old-timers," one man with a scraggly beard said.

"Sure does. That just ain't right," the other man, who had twitchy eyes and hands, said. The look on both their faces told Becky she needed to get out of there and drag Herbert with her.

"That's not what's going on at all. Becky, are you all right? Who's this guy?" Herbert pointed at the body on the ground still partially pinning Becky's feet. He almost completely ignored the bearded man and his sidekick, Twitchy, not realizing the danger he was in.

"Get out of here, Herbert," Becky hissed.

"Yeah. Let's go." Herbert reached out his hand to help Becky up. She grabbed it tightly, got to her feet, and tried to yank him with her, but it was too late.

"You ain't going nowhere, doughboy," Twitchy said and grabbed Herbert by the shoulders. Herbert whirled around, ready to fight, and slugged the guy in the jaw. It barely fazed him. Overhead lightning flashed, and thunder quickly followed, making Becky jump.

"Run, Becky!" Herbert yelled.

"Herbert, no!"

"Get Teddy and Steve!" Herbert's arms flew. He was an excellent fighter for a guy his size, and for a minute Becky thought he'd gotten the upper hand. She took that chance, turned, and ran for help. It felt like the path between the tents stretched on for miles. Her friends were right at the edge, Martha and Fanny holding Stephen's jacket over their heads as the rain continued to fall.

"Help!" Becky shouted as another crack of thunder nearly drowned out her words.

"Becky! You look like a bone a bulldog chewed!" Martha gasped as she hurried to her friend's side, yanking the jacket away from Fanny to wrap around Becky's shoulders.

"Herbert's in trouble," she cried and pointed. Without hesitating, Stephen dashed down the pathway.

"You ladies go home," Teddy ordered.

"But Herbert..." Becky started.

"We'll get the ol' boy. The cavalry's coming." Teddy looked at Martha, who nodded.

"Come on, Becky. We're getting soaked. The boys will handle everything. Let's get on home. They'll meet us there," Martha said firmly. "Fanny, let's go."

"Oh, this is a dilly of a shower. I do hope we don't run into a twister on the way," Fanny huffed. "That would be just my luck. Oh, my hair is going to be ruined for days. Not to mention these shoes. They were a gift from one of the poshest shops in Paris. I'll never be able to wear them again."

Martha pulled Becky closer, wrapped her arm around her shoulder, and whispered, "What happened in there?"

"It-it was the Veros," Becky stammered.

"You found them. Good. Were they okay? Were you able to stop the attack? Did you get a good look at the palooka who's been pumping off all the homeless people?" Martha blathered before realizing her friend was ghostly white even under the darkness of the cloudy night sky and tree-lined path home.

"It was them. They changed, Martha. They turned into something so horrible. They're the ones killing these people. They are trading something with them, and if they can't pay, they kill them. Those harmless-looking geezers form the old country are something evil. I saw, Martha. I saw it with my own eyes."

All the while they were walking, Fanny muttered to herself about the state of her dress and hair, how she'd never wanted to walk to the carnival, and how she didn't even get a stuffed animal.

"What are we going to do?" Martha asked.

"I don't know," Becky replied. It was true. Her mind had stopped working when she saw the scales on the Veros' bare feet. What could they be? What kind of creature does what they do?

There were only two people who Becky could go to for help. Cecelia and her mother would know what to do. They'd be able to help. Surely somewhere in their books or tea leaves or family photos, they'd know what the Veros were and what to do to stop them.

Don't forget those geezers are after you too. They want you to become part of their gang, and you wouldn't be an equal partner. The thought made Becky shiver. What would they do to get their hands on her? Who would they hurt?

Finally, the MacKenzie plantation could be seen through the leaves of the trees, hurricane lamps on the front porch swaying as the wind blew. It was a thunderstorm. But luckily, Fanny's mention of a twister didn't come to fruition.

Once they were on the front porch, Kitty and Judge appeared through the front door, chuckling at the kids, who resembled wet kittens.

"Where are the boys?" Kitty asked as she brought towels and blankets to the girls to dry off with on the porch so that they didn't track in a river's worth of water.

"They'll be along," Martha said. "They got into a little bit of a row. You know how delicate the masculine ego is. Just a way to let off some steam."

How Martha could chirp so happily, Becky didn't know. Her stomach was all in knots as she stared down the dirt driveway, waiting to see the headlights to Herbert's Flivver. After the rain had stopped and two cups of hot coffee with a little brandy had been consumed, she still didn't see them.

CHAPTER 17

*B*ecky woke up still in her slip from the night before, her nylon stockings shredded. There was a pounding in her head that didn't come from a night of tripping the light fantastic. As the previous night's events came crashing back, she remembered the love tap on the back of her head when she fell to the ground and the strange homeless gent with no pulse landed on top of her. Then, she remembered Herbert. Her heart jumped to her throat. Without thinking, she left her room and dashed downstairs to find Martha at the dining room table with Judge and Kitty.

"Did the boys come home?" Becky asked, her mouth dry.

Martha shook her head no.

"My goodness, Rebecca. Where is your wrap? You shouldn't be parading around in your underthings. What if a courier comes by or one of the hired hands? Go upstairs and get something to cover yourself," Kitty said with a gasp.

"Oh boy," Becky huffed. "We've got to go find them. Do you think they're still at the carnival grounds?"

"The carnival has pulled up stakes," Judge replied from behind his newspaper. "Saw it this morning when I was in the lower forty."

Martha looked at Becky. "I'll phone the Rockdale house."

"I'll get dressed," Becky replied and turned to rush up the stairs. Before her foot hit the landing, she stopped and held her breath. The sound of a car was coming up the driveway. It had to be Herbert's. It didn't have the same clang as Teddy's.

"Is that…?" Martha had frozen in place too.

"Rebecca Madeline, what did I tell you? Hurry and get yourself decent before whoever is driving up catches you in such a scandalous disposition," Kitty hissed.

Torn between being decent and the overwhelming worry, Becky opted for the former and dashed upstairs. Fanny, having heard a car approaching, didn't waste any time getting herself together and powdering her nose as if she woke up that way.

"Who's visiting at such an hour? Why, I've barely a chance to look presentable," she said while patting her hair in place.

"Get out of the way," Becky replied as she pushed her way past her cousin, getting a grunt and gasp in response.

"You've got the manners of a bulldog, Becky."

"You've got the face of one," Becky replied before slamming her door shut.

Within minutes she was dressed in a pair of trousers that her mother despised and a blouse with a short tie around the collar. Her hair was tucked up into a cabbie hat, and her shoes were flat and good for hurrying.

When she got downstairs, it was Teddy and Stephen standing in the parlor talking with Martha.

"Am I glad to see you boys," Becky gushed. "What happened last night?"

"Well, it was quite a show. My jaw is still singing from a right jab from a bum with the DTs," Stephen said, rubbing a purple spot on his chin.

"Yeah. I'm not sure where those fellas came from, but the two of them were almost too much for the three of us to handle. It was one for the history books," Teddy replied.

"Where's Herbert?" Becky smiled, remembering how he'd come to her rescue more than once before and looked forward to hearing what sort of damage he inflicted on the hoodlums.

"Yeah, uh... Becky. Herbert is in the hospital," Stephen said. Becky put her hand to her throat. "By the time we'd gotten to him, one of those bums had him pinned while the other was doing a number. I tried not to like the guy when I found out he was part of your mother's latest matchmaking effort. But it was impossible. He's top drawer."

"What?" Becky's eyes filled with tears.

"They worked him over pretty good, Beck. But he was talking, even joking when we got him to the doctor," Teddy added. "And he asked if you were okay."

All it took was a look and everyone, even Fanny, had piled into the Ford and headed to the hospital. There was a policeman sipping a cup of joe outside Herbert's room when Becky arrived with everyone.

"Excuse me, miss. Where are you going?" the officer said as he stepped in front of the door.

"That's my friend in there. Herbert Coleman. I need to see him," she said, squaring her shoulders and ready to argue, stomp, and scream if she had to to get her way.

"Mr. Coleman barely made it in here alive. What do you know about it?" the officer asked.

"Plenty. I know the people involved. Their name is Vero. Mr. and Mrs. Vero. They live on Bryn Mawr, right by the apothecary," Becky blurted out.

"You saw them at the scene?" the officer said before rocking back on his heels.

"Yes. They were there. And they had these two thugs with them who hurt Mr. Coleman and my friends. Why are you wasting time here? You should be looking for them," Becky snapped.

"Are you sure the name is Vero?" the officer said.

"Positive," Becky replied.

"That's interesting, because a Mr. and Mrs. Vero have already talked to police about an incident last night where they say they were accosted by a woman they knew and her boyfriend, and if it wasn't for the Good Samaritans, two homeless fellows, they'd have ended up in the headlines of the local newspaper."

The officer wore a neat and crisp uniform, and his badge shined, highlighting his name. Shoemacher.

"Are you related to Daniel Shoemacher?" The

words just tumbled out of her mouth before she could weigh whether or not to mention anything.

"Danny's my cousin. Two years older. Why?"

"Please. Ask him about Becky MacKenzie. That's me. He'll tell you," she whispered.

"He'll tell me what?"

"He'll tell you that there is no way any of my friends could have hurt anyone. They were defending me. It's the Veros who... aren't on the up-and-up. Just ask your cousin. Please. People's lives could be in danger. Didn't Herbert tell you what happened? He came to help me. He wasn't looking for any trouble." Becky swallowed hard and waited for the officer to reply. Her stomach sank as he shifted from one foot to the other then rubbed the back of his neck.

"You stay right here. I'll get Danny on the blower."

When the officer disappeared around the corner to call the precinct, Becky darted into the room. There were a couple of guys lying in their own beds there in various stages of distress. Unfortunately, Herbert looked the worst with his arm in a cast and half of his face swollen and scratched like he'd been pushed into the dirt. Becky crept up to the bed and looked at his hands, red around the knuckles. *At least he got a few licks in,* she thought. Carefully, she slipped her small hand beneath his meaty mitt and squeezed.

She saw the bag of clear liquid hanging on what looked like a silver metal coat rack. She looked around the room again. The other patients didn't pay her any attention.

"This is a fine pickle I've put you in," she muttered. "Herbert, I'm so sorry. None of this would have happened if I didn't drag you into it."

Without letting go of his hand she used her foot to pull the chair next to the bed closer to her. She took a seat and wondered what to do next.

After a few minutes of the guilt wrapping her up tight, she put her head down.

"Hey, dollface. You get the number of the truck that ran over me?" Herbert said. Becky snapped her head up, looked at Herbert, and smiled.

"I'm glad to see they didn't permanently crack your melon," she said as she took his hand in both of hers.

"This thing is like a rock," he said and tapped his temple.

"Herbert, I'm so sorry. I should have never..."

"Never what? It's not your fault those two Brunos did a tap dance on my face." Herbert smiled then winced, making Becky chuckle. "What did you expect me to do? Let them rough *you* up? Not on your life, sister."

"You really are the cat's pajamas, Herbert," Becky replied.

"Aw, shucks. But did you see... no. Never mind," Herbert said.

"What?"

"No. I was seeing things. The rain was heavy and didn't help us, did it?" Herbert chortled.

"What did you see?" Becky leaned forward.

"Like I said, it was just the rain. It was dark in that corridor. Plus, Teddy had a flask, and I enjoyed a couple nips that..."

"Herbert, please. Tell me what you saw." Becky squeezed his hand tightly, making him wince again.

"Snakes." Becky held her breath. "Man... sized... snakes."

Becky swallowed hard. A shiver ran across her shoulders. Her hands went clammy. "You saw them too. It's the Veros. They aren't... normal."

"No, Becky. It was my eyes playing tricks on me. It was dark and raining and..."

"No! I saw them too. I see lots of things, Herbert. Your eyes weren't playing tricks on you. It was real. What you saw was real. Look, I know it sounds like horsefeathers, but here's the straight skinny." Becky gave Herbert a condensed explanation of what was going on. Without going into detail about her encounters with the spirits still roaming Savannah long after they'd died, Becky told him about the Veros wearing no shoes, how she saw their feet change, and that they were responsible for the murders that were going on in the city.

"They're preying on these homeless people. I can only assume because they think no one cares about them. No one deserves to be snuffed out like this. We've got to get you out of here. Then we can make a plan and..." Herbert gently put a swollen finger against Becky's lips.

"Hold on, dollface. Do you hear what you're saying?"

Becky let out a long deep breath. What did she expect? That Herbert was so enraptured by her that he'd just swallow what she said hook, line, and sinker? Yes. That was exactly what she thought.

"You've got to trust me," Becky pleaded.

"Look, Becky, you really are top drawer. But in case you didn't notice, I'm in no condition to get back in the ring. Not to mention that I'm connected to this contraption for a reason. Although I'm not sure what it is," he joked as he tugged on the tube of liquid hooked to his arm.

"Right. Of course," Becky said, only to feel she'd said too much.

She'd waited years to tell Martha and Teddy about her special talents for seeing things other people didn't. Talking to ghosts in the cemetery. Seeing premonitions of things to come. Sometimes even getting a glimpse of a scandal or two upon shaking someone's hand or hearing their voice. She'd carefully sat Adam down and explained things to him and waited for his response with nervous fidgeting and a gut feeling he wasn't going to understand. But he did. Now she'd blurted this theory out to Herbert as if she was doing nothing but telling him she had a severe case of poison ivy. What was she thinking? Why did she just do this and sabotage her chances with the nicest fella she'd met in a long time? Why did she just assume he'd want to stick his neck out again when the last time he did, he got a first-class ticket to the croaker?

Before she could apologize for everything and try to walk back all the information she'd spilled, the gang and one angry copper came into the room.

"I told you, Miss MacKenzie, that you were not to come in this room. Come on. Visiting hours are over," Officer Shoemacher said. This was not the friendly Shoemacher either.

"Hey, flatfoot. Give the lady a break. She ain't bothering no one," Herbert said. Teddy, Martha, and Stephen stood behind the officer, looking like they all might need to make a break for the door any second.

"Oh yeah? Well, she's bothering me. Come on, young lady." The officer walked up and extended one hand while holding the door open with the other.

"You did see what you think you did," Becky whispered as she leaned in and gave Herbert a kiss on the cheek. Even with his face roughed up and swollen, he smelled good. When she pulled back, he winked at her, sending her emotions to the brims of her eyes in a wave of tears she managed to hold back.

"If that's true, I don't think Savannah is a place for either one of us," he whispered back.

It sounded like a good-bye of sorts. But Becky wasn't going to let herself believe that. Herbert wouldn't skip out on her. He was a good egg. Only cowards and cheaters ran away without saying good-bye. It was the first time she thought of Adam that way, even if she hadn't admitted it to herself. The healing process had advanced. She was no longer so sad. She was angry. Angry that he left her the way he did and that he made no attempt at all, not even a letter, to try to explain himself. Herbert wasn't like Adam at all. They were night and day. He wouldn't leave without saying good-bye. She was sure of it.

Before he could slap the cuffs on her and drag her from the room, Officer Shoemacher cleared his throat. "If we could speed things along."

"I'm coming," Becky said and hurried to join her friends. Out in the hallway, a couple of nurses in starched white dresses shuffled past, making their rounds. One with similar red hair like Becky's slipped into Herbert's room. She was just his type, Becky thought for a moment but then shoved the thought away. She hadn't hung her sign on him. Not to mention she had more important things to focus on.

"Did you call your cousin?" Becky asked Officer Shoemacher. "Did you ask him about me? He told you, right? He told you we weren't trouble, didn't he?"

"He told me to bring you down to the station," Officer Shoemacher said before clearing his throat.

"What? What for?" Martha stepped in before

Becky, who planted her hands on her hips. She couldn't let her temper get the best of her.

"The Veros mentioned her name in a complaint," Officer Shoemacher said.

"That's a lot of bunk," Teddy barked.

"Becky was almost attacked last night," Stephen said. "The man laid up in that bed took on the hooligans that could have killed her. Just ask him."

"I did. He said he didn't remember much of anything. All he knew was he was looking for Rebecca MacKenzie, who he'd seen slip between the two tents. Not a safe place for man or woman."

Suddenly it felt like the middle of Becky's chest had fallen out. Why, that yellow-bellied jobbie. If anyone understood clamming up over what the Veros really were, it was Becky. But to say nothing, leaving anyone to make up a yarn about her—well, that changed everything. Of course, he didn't have to say what he saw. Two old folks that turned into some kind of snake creatures wasn't something you saw unless you were suffering the DTs.

"Look here, copper. I'm not leaving town any time soon," Becky squawked. "Can you let me at least tell my parents what is going on so my father can come with me to the station?"

Everyone was quiet. Aside from the soft swoosh

of a big habited nun who was walking with her hands folded, muttering as she rolled rosary beads between her fingers, there wasn't a single sound.

"All right," the officer said reluctantly as he puffed out his chest. "But if you ain't at the precinct by this afternoon, there will be trouble."

Without saying another word, Martha took Becky by the hand and pulled her down the corridor as Becky thanked the officer and promised to be there.

"What is Uncle Judge going to say?" Martha muttered. "And poor Aunt Kitty is going to think your face is on wanted sheets in every post office across the South."

"I'm not going home. Not yet," Becky said. As they hurried down the corridor, Becky spotted Fanny chatting with a man in a long white coat and a stethoscope around his neck.

"There's my cousin now," Fanny said with a roll of her eyes.

"Becky!" the doctor chirped happily. "Where are you going in such a hurry? How about a dance at Willie's tonight?"

"Sorry, Charlie. Not tonight." Becky smiled and waved as she hurried with Martha out the front door.

"How do you know her?" Fanny snapped.

"Everybody who's anybody knows Becky. She's one of the sweetest charms around. How do you know her?" Charlie the doctor asked, only to get a huff and eye roll before Fanny turned and joined Stephen and Teddy as they followed the girls. Once everyone was piled in the car, Becky asked to be taken to Bryn Mawr Avenue.

"The only one who might have a clue as to what we're dealing with is Cecelia." Becky looked at Stephen, who was driving Herbert's car. With a wink, they were off. Fanny complained all the way as Martha listened to Teddy talk about how they found two ne'er-do-wells going to town on Herbert.

"When they saw us coming, they skedaddled," Teddy added. "Funny how evening the score made them turn tail."

Becky put her hand to her chest. Poor Herbert. Although she was bent completely out of shape over his own lack of courage telling the police that the Veros were there, she hated the thought of him being sucker-punched like that. He did, after all, come to help Becky and told the copper that much. Still, he turned out to be not quite the man she thought he was.

"I can't believe you are going to see that gypsy

again. There are quite a few people around town who have seen you in that dirty apothecary, and word has traveled back to your mother," Fanny said.

"I'm not asking you to come with. And the apothecary isn't dirty. It's eclectic, and not all medicines and perfumes come in fancy bottles. Some come in roots and ground-up spices." Becky wondered why Fanny was even in the car with them. "It's not a department store, Fanny."

"All I know is when I was in Paris, such places were avoided at all costs, lest you catch more than just a bad reputation," Fanny huffed before patting her hair in place and smiling at a man giving her the once-over as the car pulled to a stop in front of Cecelia's building.

CHAPTER 18

Becky told her friends to go home. She'd hop a cab back. But she made them all swear not to say a word to Kitty or Judge until she got back.

"I don't see how you can expect us to remain quiet about such a thing. You are wanted by the police," Fanny huffed, itching to get her cousin in more trouble.

"She isn't *wanted* by the police," Martha snapped. "They just want to talk to her. That's a lot different from slapping her in a set of silver bracelets."

"Fanny won't say anything," Stephen said. "A woman with a secret is an attractive thing. It shows in her eyes."

Fanny fell hook, line, and sinker for the ruse,

making Becky wonder how such a dumb person could be the favorite of the family. But, grateful for his help, Becky patted Stephen's hand before hurrying into the apothecary. She heard the car pull away behind her as the bells over the door jingled overhead. What she saw inside made her gasp.

There was a darkness throughout the place. Becky looked out the window to see if a set of thick clouds hadn't just skirted past the sun. But outside the sun was shining bright. The air felt humid inside, and there was a faint smell that was unfamiliar to Becky. Nothing like the roots and leaves and spices she was used to smelling. Something somewhere had gone off.

Before Becky could call for anyone, she heard stomping down the stairs. A wild-eyed Ophelia appeared with a double-barrel shotgun pointed at the door. Her hair was even more wild than usual, like she hadn't combed it for days, and her eyes were sunken and red.

"Ophelia?" Becky's hands shot up in the surrender pose.

"Oh, Becky," Ophelia gasped. She lowered the gun and shook her head. "I thought they'd come back."

"Who? What's going on in here?"

"The Veros. Come." Ophelia waved Becky up with one hand after hoisting the shotgun over her shoulder. When Becky made it to their small apartment at the top of the stairs, skirting past the candles glowing on the landings, her heart nearly stopped.

"What happened?" was all she could ask.

"They've cursed her. We know what they are. I saw it in the tea leaves. There was an awful smell about them. Evil smell. But they won't come at me. Cowards. They chose to hobble me through my beautiful daughter." Ophelia's eyes filled with tears. Becky had always seen Ophelia as a hardened old broad. She and Cecelia had reminded her of business partners more than mother and daughter. But in an instant, she saw how much love this mother had for her daughter. It made Becky think of Kitty. How could it not?

"Ophelia? What are they?"

"They are *Blutbad*. People who change their shapes and do the devil's work." Ophelia pulled a worn kerchief from her pocket and wiped her nose.

"If I hadn't seen it myself, I'd say you were off your rocker. But I've seen it. Snakes. Can I see Cecelia?" Becky asked.

She took a deep breath. The apartment was stuffy, even though the windows were open. A small fan whirred in the corner but barely disturbed the heavy air. Becky was sure some of this stifling atmosphere was due to whatever the Veros had brought upon their neighbor.

"She won't recognize you. She has a fever," Ophelia said.

Becky walked into the tiny bedroom that was really nothing more than a corner of the apartment separated from the rest by a thick curtain. Cecelia was lying on a small wrought-iron-frame bed. Her cheeks were flushed red with fever. Her skin glistened with sickly perspiration. And her hair that was normally shiny and sparkled with highlights of silver was dull and matted. Becky swallowed hard as she walked up to the bed. The heat radiated from Cecelia's body, and there was the sour smell of illness around her. Tears surfaced in Becky's eyes. Without saying a word, she whirled around and walked to the window where so many times the women had shared tea. Cecelia was like a guardian angel. Someone who Becky had gone to over and over for help and advice. She knew all about Becky's gifts and gave meaning to them. What would she do if Cecelia didn't recover?

"What do the Veros want from you, Ophelia?"

The old sage gazed with worry at her sleeping

daughter. Then she looked at Becky. Even her eye, white with cataracts, blazed with anger.

"They buy the building next door. It was no good from the start. They let the hobos come stay there. Those people bring their own kind of bad with them. But the ignorant fools think they've found a safe place. Shelter. Some bread to eat. Little do they know," Ophelia said.

"Little do they know what?"

"The Veros take their belongings. They call them family. Relatives. Earn their trust. Only to hunt them down at night in their true form and devour them from the inside out," Ophelia said, her English slightly broken.

"From the inside out?"

"A man can't live without his blood. They suck it out like the vampires made up in stories. In order to do that, they have to revert to their real form. The same as the Deceiver in the Garden of Eden," Ophelia replied. "Then, they get money. Money for the deaths. Legal papers are signed, and they get money for their deaths. To desecrate the dead one more time."

Becky thought for a moment. "I've heard of that. My father has that, and all his hands in the fields in case they get hurt on the job. The Equitable Life

Assurance Society will pay the family... if a person dies."

Becky felt sick to her stomach. The Veros lived like paupers but were making money on the murders of these homeless men and women. As if that weren't bad enough, they were *committing* the murders. It was obvious to Becky that this was an organized scheme. The Veros weren't just monsters; they were experienced, skilled monsters who had probably passed off as innocent greenhorns fresh off the boat all the way from Ellis Island to the city of Savannah and everywhere in between. What could *she* do? There was no way she could concentrate in the stifling apartment. She walked over to the open window and stepped around the flowerpots growing exotic herbs and medicinal flowers and out onto the fire escape. Even though it was a sultry summer day, the air felt not only cooler but cleaner than it was inside.

After a few deep breaths, Becky leaned against the rail and looked around. What was she going to do? She couldn't sit by and let Cecelia get sicker or let Ophelia be muscled into participating in this grisly scheme.

"Think, Rebecca," she muttered, but nothing came. Her mind was a complete blank. Had she been required to come up with a place to have a nip, she could do it within seconds. But to help her friend in a pinch, it was like she barely knew how to spell her own name.

When she looked down the alley, about to go back inside to tell Ophelia she didn't know what to do, she saw the Veros. They were urging a woman in a dowdy coat and a knitted cap on her head, even though it was hot outside, into their complex. *Their next victim*, Becky thought.

Without thinking, she climbed carefully down the fire escape and crept up to the building. Ophelia was right. It was no good. Becky could feel it. It was a two-flat squeezed in between an abandoned building with a For Rent sign in the window and a men's shoe shop that was only open during the day. Becky hadn't noticed it planted next to the apothecary, but why would she? It was men's shoes.

The back door had been closed, but Becky didn't let that stop her. She took hold of the knob, gave it a twist, and waited for it to be stopped by the lock in place. It never did. The door opened. Looking over her shoulder, Becky realized that even in the broad daylight, she was trembling.

What are you going to do once you are in there? her

conscience needled. She ignored it and stepped inside.

Down the hall, the voices of the Veros could be easily recognized. The woman they'd escorted in made no sound at all.

"You see, we want to help. You sign this paper. This will protect you in case you are hurt," Mr. Vero said in his heavy accent.

"Yes, you'll have a place to stay off the streets. We don't have much food, but you'll have something to put in your belly. All you must do is sign," Mrs. Vero encouraged in the soft, kind voice Becky had heard come out of her mouth the first time they met. Strange, but it had a hypnotic sound to it. Becky listened intently, unaware she was slowly leaning in, her feet tiptoeing to catch up with her torso.

She came upon a quaint sitting room, scarcely decorated but cozy nonetheless. The woman in the frumpy coat and knit cap had her back to Becky as she sat, slowly rocking from side to side like a child, on an ottoman at the end of an armchair. Mrs. Vero was sitting in the chair with her hand firmly on the woman's shoulder.

In front of her, Mr. Vero paced casually back and forth. But it wasn't because of nervous energy. Nor was it because he was impatient. Becky saw what he was doing without being the focus of his attention. The frumpy woman was watching him, her body moving in unison with his like she was under a spell. He was hypnotizing her like a king cobra might do to its prey before striking. Mr. Vero looked at the woman with unblinking eyes. Becky wondered if the poor soul didn't think he was seeing her like no one else had and met his gaze feeling a comforting effect. It was sick. The woman had no idea what they were doing to her.

Mrs. Vero handed the young woman a pen and held a document in front of her. Of course, she'd sign it if she knew how to spell. Otherwise, an *X* would suffice.

"Just sign," Mrs. Vero encouraged.

"You can come and go as you please. This is now your home. We'll hold your things safe. You can trust us," Mr. Vero said. As he did, Becky saw a shadow fall over his face. His features began to change, stretch, shift. He licked his lips, and a long serpent's tongue crossed over an eye and slid across his nose before he retracted it back into his mouth.

Becky gasped. The Veros turned and glared at her. She'd gotten so caught up in this gross display she hadn't realized she'd walked right into view. The bag lady they'd lured into their home stayed seated but stopped rocking and shook her head.

"You!" Mrs. Vero shouted, her lips curling over pink gums with two pointed fangs at the corners. The same that could have caused the puncture wounds on Crazy Mary and the poor fellows who had fallen into their trap. When she looked at Mr. Vero, it wasn't the fangs that stood out as much as the scales on his face and his claws. Like the paws of an alligator, strong enough to swat a melon clean off the shoulders.

"I know w-what you are," Becky stammered. "*Blutbad!*"

Mrs. Vero recoiled at the sound of the name like it hurt her ears. But in a split second, she was in a rage and stood up, her body stretching and morphing into something that was human only in the barest sense of having two arms and two legs and walking upright.

Mr. Vero knocked the bag woman to the floor, stepping over her like she was nothing more than a pile of laundry. Becky shuffled backward and collided into the wall. There was no slipping to the left or the right. She was trapped.

"And we know what you are," Mrs. Vero hissed from behind her monstrous husband, who threw his shadow over Becky as he came ever closer. "*Clar-vazator!*"

"You're cracked!" Becky yelped. "I don't know what you're talking about. I don't know what that word means. You've been out in the sun too long."

She didn't register half the things she was saying. Nervous blathering was all it was, and she just let it pour out of her mouth. Somehow, the sound of her own voice gave her strength. It reminded her that she was just a woman in Savannah who liked dancing and having a nip now and again. She adored her friends, and who knew what was going to happen with Herbert or if Adam would ever come back. She wanted her mother and father. It suddenly dawned on her that her life was passing before her eyes.

Just as the Veros were about to close in, Becky saw the woman they'd convinced to enter their lair step meekly behind them. Only when the crash was heard, and Mr. Vero crumpled to the floor, did Becky realize she'd smashed a lamp over his head.

"You crazy biddy!" Mrs. Vero scolded and lunged at the woman, who let out a scream so loud it made Becky's teeth vibrate. She had her by the throat, her fangs bared in a fit of rage. With her mouth stretched unnaturally wide, Mrs. Vero was about to do to this lady what she'd done to Crazy Mary. Becky shut her eyes. She couldn't bear to watch. Just then the front door was kicked in, and a familiar face in a blue uniform came charging in.

"Hold it right there!" Officer Daniel Shoemacher shouted with his cousin and another flatfoot behind him. Becky snapped her eyes wide open and nearly laughed out loud with relief.

The scene they walked into was Mrs. Vero towering over the babbling homeless woman, Mr. Vero unconscious on the floor, and Becky cowering against the wall. Within seconds Mrs. Vero turned back into the innocent old lady, acting shaken and confused. Fortunately, Officer Shoemacher wasn't buying it.

"Put your hands where we can see them! Don't do anything funny!" he shouted.

"What? What's this all about? You see, Officer, what they've done to my husband." Mrs. Vero tried to manipulate the coppers, but they weren't having any of it. In fact, as Becky watched her fangs retract, leaving only a thin trail of drool over her chin, and her scaly skin return to thin, papery, old-lady skin, she waited for the officers to gasp in disbelief. They never did. They couldn't see it. Only Becky could.

And maybe, just maybe the homeless woman could see what they were too.

It was too much. As the police raced in and separated Mrs. Vero from her husband, Becky watched them put a set of handcuffs on her. They didn't seem at all afraid she might bite them or worse. They talked to her like she was nothing more than an old lady caught breaking the law.

"What are you trying to do, Rona? Give Ma Barker a run for her money?" Officer Shoemacher asked as he led her out the door. She didn't even look at Becky. Not even out of the side of her eye.

The other officer tended to the homeless woman as the third waited for the whitecoats to come and pick up Mr. Vero.

"This one can go on ice," he said to the second Officer Shoemacher.

"Dead?"

"As a doornail."

Becky remained where she was pressed against the door. It was only when Stephen Penbroke came rushing through the door that she dared take a step forward before everything went black. He'd sped back to the apothecary.

"When I saw you wasn't there, Ophelia told me

you'd gone down the fire escape and in the direction of the Veros' building. What were you thinking going into some strange house all alone? The police were already at your house. Funny, both Officer Shoemachers seemed to know something was up too. Your reputation is getting around, Rebecca," Stephen scolded as he helped her get her legs underneath her again.

"So, this means I owe you one," Becky muttered.

"That you do," Stephen replied.

CHAPTER 19

"*B*ecky, that dress is the cat's meow," Martha said as she ran up to her best friend as soon as she saw her pull up in front of the Potts' grand home. It was their end-of-summer picnic. There were banners and balloons as far as the eye could see. People were playing games of potato sack races, horseshoes, and pin the tail on the donkey.

Becky smiled and gave a turn, causing the green dress she was wearing to flounce up elegantly, exposing her new stockings without a single run in them.

"Mama picked it out," she said as Kitty and Judge got out of the car, linked arms, and sauntered up the grassy hill to the front porch that wrapped all the way around the house. People called their names, and everyone who was anyone in Savannah was there. Even Cecelia was supposed to make an appearance, since she was a very hot commodity among the elite of Savannah for her tarot readings. But she'd declined, telling the Potts she was psychically exhausted from a trip to Baton Rouge and a séance that had gone awry. No one questioned her. The truth was she was on the mend from the Veros' whammy. Mr. Vero had been the warlock who tried to strong-arm Ophelia. Now that he was dead, so was his curse.

"I've been waiting for you. So, you didn't bring a beau?" Martha whispered.

"She's scared off everyone this side of the Mason-Dixon," Fanny huffed as she pulled a pink lace fan from her clutch, which matched her dress. Everyone wearing a set of full-length trousers looked in her direction as she sauntered up the walk just a step behind Becky and Martha.

"Fanny, could you dummy up for a change?" Becky sighed. "Your mouth has been running nonstop like someone slipped a nickel in you."

"Besides, I wouldn't say that, Cousin Fanny." Martha linked her arm through Becky's. "There is a very handsome gentleman out at the gazebo who has been earnestly waiting for you."

"Who is it?" Fanny asked before Becky could.

"A Mr. Herbert Coleman. And I might add he is looking as dapper as can be. An alderman or not, that fella knows how to dress," Martha chirped before she jerked her head in the direction of the gazebo in the Potts' backyard.

Becky didn't say a word after she gave Martha a peck on the cheek. Then she slowly strolled through the guests, saying hello to everyone and grabbing herself a glass of punch before zeroing in on Herbert. She hadn't seen him since her visit in the hospital. Although her feelings had altered slightly since he wouldn't admit that he saw the Veros' monstrous side, she'd found she missed him anyway. He was a good egg.

She wondered if he'd heard through the grapevine about the Veros. Luckily, Mr. Vero died from his injuries inflicted by the homeless woman, whose name was Edith Lefold. Miss Lefold had some issues in her head and had been romancing the streets for months. Her family heard about the incident and quickly gathered her up and absconded with her back to Atlanta, where she could get some help. No charges had been brought against her. Unlike Mrs. Vero.

Just as the police had raided the place and got Mrs. Vero in custody, Becky had fainted. As it turned out, no one had seen Mr. Vero or Mrs. Vero in any of their shapeshifting. None of the police saw her fangs, her scaly feet, or Mr. Vero's abnormal forked tongue. Only Becky saw it. She saw it in her dreams, and she saw it in *her* reality. The reality that brought ghosts to the dinner table and specters along on dates.

Mrs. Vero, however, was arrested. As it turned out, there was a long trail of bodies following the innocent old couple. They'd started their killing spree in Little France, also known as Louisiana. New Orleans, to be exact. That only stood to reason, since the town itself boasted the languages of hoodoo and voodoo.

But Mrs. Vero and her deceased husband had also been cheating several businesses, claiming their relatives, who were, in fact, innocent homeless individuals, had perished mercilessly at the hands of a lunatic. Money was paid out for the untimely deaths to the tune of almost four hundred thousand dollars. The Veros—*Blutbads*, shapeshifters, whatever they were—would travel like their ancestors, gather signatures from people on the skids, then move on to the next town. By the time they circled back to the first set of hobos, enough time on their policies would have gone by and the bean counters wouldn't think anything of it except that it was an unfortunate death. To the regular world, they were low-grade con artists. But Becky knew what they really were. She'd seen them. And one other person had seen it too.

Herbert was standing in the gazebo, eating from a plate piled high with cake. The sight made her smile wide. But she held herself in check. Slowly, she sipped her punch as she sauntered to the gazebo. When Herbert finally caught sight of her, he set his plate down, smoothed his tie, and smiled wide.

"Green always was my favorite color," he said.

"You are a sight for sore eyes," Becky replied. "How are you feeling?"

"Right as rain. It'll take a little more than a couple of busters to take me down. I will say that what nearly did me in was I only got one visit from my favorite dollface. I wasn't sure if I was going to recover from that." Herbert winked.

"Oh, Herbert. I am sorry. You heard about what happened, the Veros, the scandal?" she asked, looking up at him, waiting for him to mention what he'd seen. Her breath hung in her chest.

"Yes. Saw it in black and white. Whatever happened to working for what you want? As a businessman, it makes me sick. I hope they throw the book at that old woman," Herbert said as if he were talking about the average, run-of-the-mill gangster.

"Yes," Becky muttered, still gazing up at him, waiting.

"Speaking of business, I'll be heading back to Mobile." He took a deep breath and let it out like he'd been holding those words in and finally felt relief saying them. Becky swallowed.

"So soon?"

"My business ain't gonna run itself," he said as he stepped closer to her. "Besides, you're as rooted here as those tobacco plants in the fields are. I don't see you skipping town any time soon."

She could smell his cologne. For a minute, she got lost in it. "Why did you mention the tobacco field?" Becky said the words after she really thought about them. The words from the hobo in the speakeasy behind the dry cleaner came rushing back to her. *Stay out of the tobacco fields.* Was Herbert trying to tell her something too?

"Just because that's where you live. It's home," Herbert replied.

"Yes. It is home. But the door is always open for visitors." Becky smiled.

"I have the feeling my conglomerates might send me back this way again sometime." Herbert smiled.

"You saw them," Becky finally whispered. They were the words she'd been dying to say. "No one else did. The police who arrested Mrs. Vero. Edith Lefold. Just us and maybe the victims. But you saw them."

"I did. But I'll never admit it to anyone else. Ever. I can't, Becky. I just can't." Herbert smirked before looking toward all the guests frolicking in the massive yard. They stood together in silence for a few seconds before Becky took his beefy paw in her delicate hands and squeezed.

"I'm going to miss you, Herbert."

"I'm going to miss you, too, Becky."

It would have been shocking and scandalous if anyone had noticed that Herbert had slipped his strong, thick arm around Becky's waist, pulled her tightly to him, and planted a kiss that only Valentino could have pulled off. However, no one noticed the pair. The games of horseshoe went on, and more food was brought from the kitchen.

Herbert said good-bye to Martha, Fanny, Teddy, and Stephen, shaking the men's hands. Becky watched him climb into his Flivver and drive off.

After talking with Martha and wiping a single tear from the corner of her eye, Becky joined the party. She had a marvelous time, ate too much food, and danced until her feet ached. Still, as the sun was setting, she asked Stephen to drive her to the edge of the tobacco fields of the MacKenzie plantation so she could walk home.

"Mind if I join you?" he asked.

"Of course not," Becky replied.

They talked and laughed and at times walked quietly. It was only when the sun was about to dip below the horizon, the sky brilliant rose and purple colors, everything in rich midnight-blue shadow that was too beautiful to be scary, that she saw something that made her heart stop. And then it was gone. Becky was sure she saw Adam a couple yards ahead before he ducked back into the rows of tobacco.

"Are you okay?" Stephen asked. "Please don't tell me you are going to faint again. You weigh a lot more than you look."

"Very funny." Becky gave his arm a swat before linking her arm through his.

ABOUT THE AUTHOR

Harper Lin is a *USA TODAY* bestselling cozy mystery author.

When she's not reading or writing, she loves hiking, doing yoga, and baking with her family and friends.

For a complete list of her books by series, visit her website.

www.HarperLin.com